When she was good, she was very, very good. But when she was bad...she was better!

"What are you doing here, lady," Tyce asked hoarsely, fitting Claire against him, "driving all these gentlemen wild?"

"Dancing," she breathed, her voice lost to the sensual feel of his hard body pressing hers into slow, rhythmic movement. A dance, only a dance, but the pleasure somehow made it more.

"Looked like you were doing more than that."

"Did it look like I was being...naughty?"

"I'd say you were headed that way."

Her lips curled in enjoyment. His gaze lowered to her mouth and lingered there intently until a serious heat washed through her. "I told you from the start," she whispered, "I want to be bad."

"Bad." He angled his face intimately toward hers. "With a man?"

"Yes. With a man."

He led her in a turn, his hand warm and controlling at the small of her back. "In case you've been too busy to notice—" his gaze intensified "—I'm a man."

Dear Reader,

In a society where movie stars, modern-day royals and billionaire heiresses are virtually hunted by celebrity seekers, I imagine that the most famous might grow lonely in their well-guarded ivory towers. They might crave a respite from their notoriety, a chance to connect with others on a more elemental plane, a brief sojourn into the life of an average Jane Doe.

What would happen to a runaway heiress, then, if while traveling incognito, she meets the one man who ignites a soul-deep passion within her, a man who gives her a lingering taste of the love she almost stopped believing existed?

In this story, Valentina Claire Richmond is just such a celebrity, pushed to the limit of her endurance and ready to risk almost anything for freedom…and the chance to love Tyce Walker.

I hope you enjoy Claire's journey as much as I did. It's surprising just how and where a "princess" on the run might find a prince in disguise.

I love to hear from readers, so please do drop me a line in care of Harlequin Books, 225 Duncan Mill Road, Don Mills, Ontario, Canada, M3B 3K9.

Sincerely,

Donna Sterling

Books by Donna Sterling

HARLEQUIN TEMPTATION
586—SOMETHING OLD, SOMETHING NEW
628—POSSESSING ELISSA
655—HIS DOUBLE, HER TROUBLE

THE PRINCESS AND THE P.I.
Donna Sterling

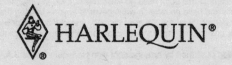

HARLEQUIN®

TORONTO • NEW YORK • LONDON
AMSTERDAM • PARIS • SYDNEY • HAMBURG
STOCKHOLM • ATHENS • TOKYO • MILAN • MADRID
PRAGUE • WARSAW • BUDAPEST • AUCKLAND

I dedicate this book to my brother Joe,
whom I love dearly.
He's true "hero material."

ISBN 0-373-25794-5

THE PRINCESS AND THE P.I.

Copyright © 1998 by Donna Fejes.

Printed in U.S.A.

Prologue

THE ONLY ADVANTAGE Claire could find in being a skinny ten-year-old was her ability to belly-crawl behind the furniture in Nanny's sitting room. At the moment, she hid behind the sofa and waited for Nanny to rise from her rocking chair, turn off the light and waddle into the kitchenette for her nightly glass of hot milk. She'd be doing so any moment now, Claire knew.

Sure enough, her plump, age-spotted hand soon reached for the lamp. The light clicked off, throwing the cozy room into darkness. The rocker groaned beneath shifting weight, then footsteps plodded into the adjoining kitchenette.

Claire remained in her hiding place until the sounds of Nanny pouring milk and warming it in the microwave gave way to footsteps headed through the far doorway.

Only then did Claire crawl out from behind the sofa and shine her flashlight on the pile of newspapers beside the rocker. With silent, nimble fingers she found what she'd come for. The tabloids. Nanny always buried the tabloids beneath the daily news to hide them from the maids—and, of course, from Claire herself. Uncle Edgar didn't approve of anyone bringing "scandal sheets" into the house.

Concealing the papers within her pajama top, she tiptoed from Nanny's apartment and threw glances over her shoulder as she walked down the carpeted corridor lined with paintings of her ancestors and other famous people. The shadowy corridors scared Claire when she was alone. She wished her cousin Johnny would have a room closer to hers, but he and his parents lived in the east wing instead of the west. Johnny was two years younger than she—and a pesky boy—but at least he was company.

She reached her own room with relief. Locking the door, she turned off the overhead light and burrowed beneath the covers of her massive canopied bed, where she unfolded the two tabloids.

As she shone her flashlight on their front pages, her conscience pricked her. She didn't like to disobey Uncle Edgar. But if she didn't read about herself in the tabloids, how would she ever know what was going on in her life? The adults wouldn't tell her, and Johnny never knew any more about the important things than she did.

As she suspected, the headlines were about her. One read, Custody Battle Over Valentina Grows Bitter.

"Valentina" was her first name, the name her mother had used for her whenever they were "in public," which meant at parties or having pictures taken. "Claire" was her middle name, the one her parents had called her at home. That was, of course, before they'd died in the car crash and Uncle Edgar had moved in. Everyone called her

"Valentina" now, except Nanny and Johnny, because she'd told them to call her Claire. No one else had listened to her request. Shaking off the sad thoughts, she studied the next headline: Poor Little Perfume Princess.

This headline confused her. She knew why they were calling her "Perfume Princess"; her grandfather had gotten rich with his perfume business, and her mother had been a movie star who made the perfume famous.

But why were they calling her "poor" when Nanny had told her she was rich? An heiress, she'd said. That meant that when she turned twenty-five, she would be given the money her father and mother had left for her. She'd read in a tabloid last week that she would get more than a billion dollars. That was quite a bit, wasn't it? So why was this headline calling her poor? She and her mother had always done "charity work" for the poor children. Was she now to be one of them?

That would be an interesting change. From stories Nanny told, Claire knew that poor children didn't have bodyguards following them whenever they left the house, and that they didn't have to run from photographers like her mother and she had. Most poor children didn't have to worry about things like kidnappers. Best of all, many lived in neighborhoods where lots of other children lived. They saw each other *every day*, and could walk to one another's houses. Might not be too bad, being one of the poor children....

Curiosity eating at her, she stretched out and propped up on her elbow to read. Both articles were about the fighting in court between her Aunt Shirley, her mother's sister, and Uncle Edgar, her father's uncle. Both wanted "custody." Nanny had told her that meant they both wanted her to live with them because they loved her. As Claire continued to read, though, she detected a slight difference in Nanny's version of the custody battle and the tabloid's version. The tabloids made it sound as if her aunt and uncle wanted her only for the billion dollars.

Did they?

A terrible uncertainty gripped her, making her hands tremble and her stomach hurt. *How could your aunt and uncle love you? They don't even know you.* When her parents had been alive, she'd seen her aunts and uncles only on holidays.

But it hurt too much to think that her only remaining family wanted her for the money. She thought back to what her mother used to say: *Don't believe what you read in the papers or see on television. It's not always true.* But sometimes it was. She'd found out about her parents' death from the nightly news.

With her throat aching from the pressure of unshed tears, Claire came out from under the covers and lay back against the pillows. Who could she ask who wouldn't lie to her? Nanny would tell her that everything was fine. She *always* said that, just to make her feel better. Claire knew she couldn't ask Uncle Edgar or Aunt Shirley, or anyone in their families, if they wanted her only for the money. It might hurt their feelings.

With a little sob, she slipped out of bed, sank to her knees and fervently prayed. *Please, God, help me know who to trust. And please, please, let someone love me.*

When she'd prayed as long and hard as she possibly could, she climbed back into bed and found the tabloid pages. A slight shudder of revulsion went through her. She wished she hadn't read them. No wonder Momma had hated them so, and Uncle Edgar forbade them in the house. Claire resolved to never read a tabloid again.

She also solemnly vowed to be very, very good, to follow all the rules and do exactly as she should...just in case God needed help in making someone love her.

IT HAD TAKEN her fifteen years from the time the question had first entered her heart to learn the truth. *She could trust no one.* No one except Johnny.

And "being good" hadn't won anyone's love. She'd followed every rule and tried her hardest to please them all—her uncle, her teachers, her trust officer, her public relations team, her body-guards, her small circle of approved friends, and in the last couple years, her fiancé. Where had all that effort gotten her?

Betrayed and humiliated on her would-be wedding day.

At least her eyes had been opened.

Still dressed in her sadly wilted wedding gown, she peered down from the hotel window into lush California gardens. "Look at them out there, Johnny. Dozens of paparazzi, circling like sharks for a kill."

"They can't get in, Claire," her cousin assured her, peering out another window. "We've rented out the entire hotel, and Uncle Edgar has guards at every door."

"Don't underestimate paparazzi," she warned. "They always find a way in." They'd hunted her like prey for years. She remembered the days when she'd tried to please even *them*. Her cooperation had only worsened their demands.

They were almost as troublesome as the faceless stalker who plied her with hate mail and anonymous phone calls, mentioning details of her private life that he'd apparently watched. He'd gone so far as to break into her New York town house and vandalize her bedroom.

Which of course necessitated more bodyguards. More eyes watching every move she made, more authority to bow to—a strain for someone who'd grown up trying to please everybody.

That had been her main problem, she realized. She'd been an approval junkie. The time had come to kick that habit.

"You need to rest, Claire," Johnny was telling her now as she paced across the hotel suite, the train of her pearl-seeded wedding gown dragging and tangling behind her. "You've had one hell of a morning, and dinner won't be any better."

An understatement. Dinner would be worse. By then, her uncle would have gathered all his forces, and they'd try to coerce her into rescheduling the wedding. "It doesn't matter what they say or do, Johnny," she informed him, squaring her jaw. "I won't marry Preston."

He sighed and sank down into an armchair. "Maybe I shouldn't have interfered this morning. You'd have been at your wedding reception by now."

"I'd have been miserable. If you hadn't shown me the article before the ceremony..." She paused, remembering how reluctant she'd been to look at the tabloid he'd thrust into her hands. Until that moment, she'd kept her resolution to never again read the tabloids. "If you hadn't shown me the article, I would have married him and regretted it. When I marry, I want...I want..." She didn't finish the statement. It sounded too corny.

She wanted her husband to love her.

"Maybe I'm asking too much," she mused. "But what about simple loyalty?" Throwing out her hands, she exclaimed, "Three out of four of my bridesmaids, Johnny!"

There wasn't much he could say to that. The tabloid photos of her intended in the arms of her so-called friends had left very little to the imagination. Preston hadn't bothered to deny the affairs. "They meant nothing to anyone," he claimed.

They'd meant a great deal to her. Even now, hours after seeing the photos, she felt the stab of betrayal.

Uncle Edgar had sided with Preston. "You can't let little things like infidelity bother you. Much more important issues are at stake."

Like your lucrative deal with his parents, she'd thought. Throughout all the years she'd been under his guardianship, her uncle hadn't been around enough to get to know her. But while managing her funds, he *had* found the time to build a fortune of his own....

"Wealth and fame like yours make you a target, Valentina," he'd told her. "It's not bad enough that you're one of the richest women in the world, but your mother was a Hollywood legend. Your face and name are known everywhere. I want to see you married to someone who can handle that pressure. Preston's family is very powerful. He's being groomed to run for the presidency someday. Your fame would be an asset."

An asset. She wanted to be more to her husband than an asset.

"And don't worry about this little scandal," he'd assured her. "It'll blow over soon enough. People will forget."

People might, but she wouldn't. At the very least, Preston's affairs had proven that he didn't love her...and that she didn't love him. She'd been more hurt by her friends' betrayals than she had been by his.

Oh, she *cared* about Preston, all right. Since their early teens, they'd been herded together with an elite group of peers to share ski trips, cruises, polo matches, yacht races and glittering social events. She'd liked him the best out of all the men in their closed little group, and had never considered going out of that group to meet others. It simply wasn't done. So she and Preston had convinced themselves they were in love.

She wished Nanny were still alive. She'd turn

to her for reassurance that everything was fine, even though it wasn't.

"Claire, are you okay?" asked Johnny.

She forced a smile for her weary-looking cousin. "Of course I am. I just have to figure out what to do with my life."

"Now?" he exclaimed with a quirk of his dark blond brow.

She laughed in spite of her despondent mood. "I suppose it *is* getting late. You look like you need a nap more than I do. You have to fly back to Boston tonight, don't you?"

He nodded, looking contrite. "I hate to leave you like this, but I have exams all week and need to study."

"Go get some rest. It'll be a long flight."

He lurched gratefully toward the door. "See you at dinner. Or should I call it, Round Two?" They shared a grim smile and he left her alone.

Or rather, as "alone" as she could be with paparazzi beneath her window, some perched in the trees with telescopic lenses, waiting to snap pictures of the bride who'd run away from her lavish Los Angeles wedding. In the next room was her public relations specialist, preparing a statement for the media that said she'd taken ill. Stationed outside her door were protection agents, and elsewhere in the hotel lurked countless other individuals who somehow governed her life, keeping everything in line, putting the best face on any situation, advising her on what to do, what to say and how to act.

She was thoroughly sick of it all—the rules, the expectations, the correct behavior. If only she could go away somewhere, *anywhere,* to be alone. Someplace where she wouldn't be recognized. To think. To heal. To decide what to do with her future.

She'd never had that kind of freedom. Ever.

The idea, once sparked, fanned into a fierce longing. *Freedom.* Freedom to do whatever she liked, without advisors, guards, stalkers, or paparazzi. Was it possible?

Her uncle and the powers-that-be would never go for it. "Too dangerous," they'd say. But what could be more damaging to her than this slow suffocation of her spirit?

She was a woman now, not a child. Twenty-five years old. She'd come into her money six months ago. Surely she could come and go as she pleased…couldn't she?

She almost laughed at that. Only if she ran away like a thief in the night and traveled incognito. She'd have to disguise herself, use false identification and get lost in some crowd.

She wasn't sure she could manage on her own, outside of her sheltered world. She'd lived her entire life so far like a delicate hothouse flower. But she wanted now to face the wind, to feel the rain. To find the sun.

She would do it!

She would go away somewhere, if only for a few weeks, and prove to herself that she *could* manage on her own. Maybe then she'd feel more prepared to take control of her life.

Though her heart raced with excitement, she reached for the phone with amazingly steady hands. "Johnny? Can you come back to my room, please? There's something I'd like to run past you."

"BUG THE PHONES of family and friends. We've got the airports, train stations and harbors covered. Fred, arrange interviews with her household staff—in *all* of her homes. Her vacation villas, too. Her uncle thinks she might be headed for one of them."

"Excuse me, Mr. Walker," his secretary interrupted from the door of the conference room as the rest of his hand-chosen team of private investigators scribbled notes, rifled through files and typed on notebook computers. "You have a visitor."

Tyce Walker of Walker Investigative & Security Services frowned. Who would drop by his office at this ungodly hour? It was six in the morning; he'd summoned his crew for an early meeting after an emergency call from Edgar Richmond last night. "Who is it?"

"Ms. Pitts."

With a soft curse, Tyce tossed down his pen and stood up. "Tell the security guard not to let her past the lobby. Just to be safe, lock every filing cabinet in my office and yours." To his staff, he muttered, "No matter what happens in the next half hour, keep a close watch on your briefcases and laptops. Hattie and her accomplices can be masters at diversionary tactics."

A grumble of agreement sounded from all corners of the room. During his wily foster mother's last visit, she'd waltzed away with a photograph of Senator Whitman cheating on his wife—a photo meant for Mrs. Whitman's eyes only. To Hattie's credit, though, she hadn't used the photo in the tabloid she owned; she'd merely blackmailed Tyce into helping her scoop another story.

She could be a real pain in the butt. He'd barred her from visiting any of his offices. He had, after all, learned his most devious surveillance techniques from her.

He'd been a streetwise punk when she'd plucked him out of his probation officer's car by the collar of his scruffy leather jacket, settled him into her Los Angeles home as her foster son and put him to work for her tabloid. By age seventeen, he'd converted his breaking-and-entering skills into a marketable trade, learning the basics of a stakeout, covert videotaping, electronic bugging and tracking. He'd found he had a talent for it, though no taste for tabloid reporting.

He now owned one of the top P.I. firms in the country, with offices in Los Angeles, Chicago, Washington, D.C., and Miami. Hattie, on the other hand, had nurtured her tabloid into a worldwide press. He wondered what story she was after now. He had a sinking feeling that he knew.

He spied her the moment the elevator doors opened. Petite and wiry, she paced across the lobby smoking a cigarette despite the No Smoking signs. She tipped her ashes into the paper coffee cup she held. As always, her short salt-and-pepper hair stuck up in odd places, and her dark pantsuit looked rumpled. He recognized the expression on her weathered face—impatience.

"What are you doing here in Chicago, Hattie? And at my office, yet. You know my offices are off-limits."

Squinting up at him through a haze of smoke, she took one last drag off her cigarette, then flicked the butt into the cup where it hissed and died in a pool of black coffee. "Don't waste my time, T.K.," she rumbled in her gruff, asthmatic voice.

Tyce had no idea why she called him "T.K." He didn't have a middle name, as far as he knew, and his last name was Walker, but from the time she'd first collared him, she'd called him T.K.

"Let's go to your office and talk," she said. "Here, get rid of this." She shoved the paper cup into his hands on her way to the elevator.

In one fluid motion he dropped the cup into a trash receptacle, grabbed Hattie's arm and turned her toward the glass front door, where the first weak rays of dawn barely filtered through the darkness. "I don't have time to talk."

"I've got a hot tip you'll want to hear."

"I don't work for you anymore, Hattie. I

haven't for seven years. Why would I want your tip?"

"It'll make us both rich. Put us in the tabloid hall of fame."

"I'm as rich as I need to be," he replied, somewhat amused, "and I didn't realize there *was* a tabloid hall of fame."

"Maybe there ain't," she conceded. "But an extra two or three million wouldn't hurt either of us." Though the determined set of her jaw was nothing out of the ordinary and her pent-up energy always hummed, he sensed a sharper edge to her enthusiasm this morning.

"Unless your tip has some direct bearing on one of my clients, I don't need to hear it. And since you have no way of knowing who my clients are—at least I *hope* you have no way of knowing who my clients are—"

"It has something to do with American royalty," she imparted. "More in particular, our own little Perfume Princess."

He'd gone perfectly still, as she'd probably known he would. He'd resigned from her tabloid over an assignment to watch Valentina Richmond.

After a moment Tyce managed a crooked half smile. "Let's go get some coffee. And, uh, talk."

They trudged out to his private parking deck in the early morning June breeze. That infamous assignment had been to cover Valentina's debutante ball—before, during and after. Hattie had been hoping for something spicy to liven up the dry society-page angle. She'd paired Tyce with one of her veteran reporters, Slick Sam Stephanovich, who thought nothing of bugging bedrooms, drilling holes through hotel room walls or climbing trees to use his telescopic lens.

That was how Tyce had first seen the girl who'd been dubbed "the Perfume Princess"— through a telescopic lens. She'd been in a seaside villa, alone in an upper-story bedroom, wearing a sheer white nightgown that clearly silhouetted every curve and valley of her slender, tanned body. Her waist-length blond hair had shimmered like candlelight around her. She'd been gazing out of a floor-to-ceiling window at the sun setting over the ocean.

Something about her had shaken Tyce to the core. He had no right to see her like this. Guilt burned through him, yet he couldn't bring himself to turn away. It wasn't until Sam tried to have a look that he was jolted to his senses. He broke the telescopic lens before handing it back to him. He didn't want anyone watching her unawares and shooting photos; didn't want to know who might be joining her in that private suite. She looked too innocent to sully. Too pure.

He'd quit the tabloid business that night and reported the paparazzi's movements to the girl's uncle.

Tyce almost laughed out loud at the memory. What a green kid he'd been, confusing a woman's wide-eyed, sensual appeal with innocence and vulnerability. He'd long since learned that the most beautiful ones, especially the wealthy and powerful, were usually hard on the inside, hiding the blackest of secrets.

"I suppose you're aware that Valentina called off her wedding last Saturday to Preston Hanover the Third, aren't you?" Hattie asked as they neared his gleaming forest-green Jaguar.

Tyce shrugged. He was aware of the canceled wedding, but only because Valentina's uncle had hired him last night to search for her. Hattie certainly didn't need to know that. "Seems I might have heard something about it."

"Her publicist put out the word that she'd gotten sick." Hattie snorted. "She probably *was* sick—from seeing those photos of loverboy doing his thing with her bridesmaids."

Tyce didn't comment as he helped Hattie into the passenger seat, then took his place behind the wheel. He supposed she was right. Then again, the ultra-wealthy were a different breed. Who knew how the hell they felt about anything?

"There's been a new development in the drama," Hattie informed him. Leaning toward him as if she were about to let him in on a great secret, she divulged, "Valentina took off for parts unknown yesterday afternoon. Alone."

He kept his face expressionless and started up the car's engine. Did Hattie know that Edgar Richmond had hired him to find her? He didn't think so. This juicy tidbit was simply the kind she loved to pursue. "Why would you think that news might interest *me?*"

"Because I'm hiring you to find her."

Tyce shot her a surprised glance. She'd badgered him for favors before, but never offered to buy his services.

"This is my ticket to the big time, T.K. Everyone will want to know why she ran away, where she went, what she's doing and who she's doing it with."

Tyce slanted her a mildly derisive glance. "You've been in the business too long, Hattie."

"Oh, come on, T.K. This is better than a prime-time soap. I'm going after the scoop, one way or another." With an understated emphasis that always signaled the dropping of a bomb, she casually let out, "But I'd rather not have to trust my reporters with the information I have about Valentina's flight."

The bomb hit home. He needed that information. And the last thing he wanted was one of her reporters finding Valentina before he did. "What about her flight?"

Hattie cracked a speculative smile, tapped a cigarette from her pack, stuck it between her teeth and leisurely flicked her lighter into a blaze. "You taking my case?"

Tyce plucked the cigarette from her mouth and pitched it out the window. She knew he didn't allow smoking in his car. Her information had to be hot; she was getting power-happy. "I charge a hefty fee."

"Charge away. I'm good for it. Now, about our runaway princess." She pulled out a cassette recorder. "She's always been closest to her cousin, John Peterson, so I had his phone tapped since the wedding fiasco. Wednesday I hit pay dirt. If I'd listened to the tape earlier, I could have had her followed from the start."

Tyce shook his head. Leave it to Hattie to have key information only hours after the goodbye note had been found. "Let's hear the tape."

"Only if I have your word that you'll find her before anyone else does. I want to know where she went, why she went there, and who she's with."

The same information her uncle wanted, of course. His gaze locked with Hattie's. He didn't want to complicate matters by bringing her in on his search. Edgar Richmond expected absolute confidentiality—and offered payment that was far more valuable to Tyce than money. On the other hand, Hattie would go elsewhere with her information if he didn't cooperate.

If he accepted her case, which would mean he'd be working for both Edgar Richmond *and* Hattie, he'd have to walk a thin line to keep their interests from conflicting. With careful timing, though, he could delay his report to Hattie until after he'd submitted his final report to Edgar.

"I'll find Valentina for you," he slowly agreed, "and supply you with the information you want, *if* you promise to stay out of my way. Let me handle the investigation. If you interfere, the agreement's off."

"Will you take pictures?"

This, as she knew damn well, was stretching it. He wasn't a photographer. "A few."

Hattie shrugged. "Okay, T.K., I'll stay out of your way. I'm too tied up with celebrity lawsuits right now to do much fieldwork anyway, and I wouldn't trust any of my reporters with a story this big. That is, unless I have to."

With grave reluctance, Tyce shook on the deal. Hattie played the taped phone conversation.

"It's about time you called. I'm late for an exam," came the young man's harried voice, to which his cousin uttered apologies. "I had some ID made for you—a driver's license and a passport—but you'll have to change your hair to red, cut it and curl it. The name is 'Claire Jones.' I thought it would be easier for you if we picked a first name you were used to."

"Yes, Claire Jones will be fine."

"Your flight's tomorrow evening. I couldn't get a direct flight, so you'll have a three-hour layover in Dallas. I've sent you the papers, tickets and plenty of cash, overnight express."

"Thanks, Johnny, but I don't want you to get in trouble."

"Don't worry, Claire, I won't. But I am concerned about you. I'm sending someone to meet you at the airport and drive you wherever you want to go."

"No! Don't send anyone. I'm sick of

guards and drivers. Besides, no one can be trusted."

"You shouldn't wander around by yourself. What if that stalker finds you? I'll hire someone who can act as a driver and a bodyguard, but I won't tell him who you really are."

"No driver, no bodyguard! Uh-oh, someone's coming. I've got to go. Don't send anyone…and don't worry about me. I won't contact you again for at least a month. They'll probably tap your phone when they know I'm gone. I can't chance them tracing me. Thanks again, Johnny."

Tyce took the tape from the recorder and slipped it into his shirt pocket. He'd have "Claire Jones's" travel route traced to her destination. She was obviously traveling east from Los Angeles, which would take quite a few hours, plus the layover her cousin had mentioned. Tyce realized that he himself might have an advantage from his central Chicago location.

With any luck at all—and his corporate jet— he'd get to her destination airport before she did.

2

SHE'D MADE HER ESCAPE during a Thursday afternoon shopping trip to an upscale mall—a touch below her usual Paris boutiques and Rodeo Drive shops, but not enough to raise eyebrows. Stopping to use a rest room, she'd hurriedly changed into her "disguise," then strode out past her bodyguards and into the real world.

The ensuing journey had proven to be a challenge. She'd had to hail a cab on a busy Los Angeles street where crowds had fought for every car. She'd waited in long lines at the airport, agonizing over the possibility of getting caught with false identification. She'd suffered wolf whistles from a rowdy bunch of young soldiers and tolerated hours of ceaseless chatter from the woman next to her on the plane.

It had been, in its own way, exhilarating.

Valentina the Perfume Princess wouldn't have been exposed to any of that. She would have traveled on her private jet with her own servants to wait on her. For that very reason, Claire gleaned perverse satisfaction from her night-long ordeal. She'd made it, at least this far, on her own.

As the plane landed at Atlanta Hartsfield International Airport, her heart drummed. She could be caught at this end of the flight and exposed as a fraud—a terrifying thought. She could have been followed by that psychotic stalker or accosted by the media. All of those possibilities left her feeling wary and vulnerable.

She bolstered her courage with one thought: if she made it through this airport unimpeded, *she'd be free.*

She shuffled through the jetway with large tortoiseshell sunglasses concealing half her face. In the place of her usual long, pale blond tresses were now loose, strawberry-blond curls that barely grazed her shoulders—a color and style that she'd actually managed to achieve by herself last night. She hoped her new hair, denim cutoffs, yellow T-shirt and sunglasses would be enough to disguise her.

As she turned the corner and approached the exit gate, she slowed to a standstill. A man with a video camera and a woman with a microphone stood eagerly examining the faces of the departing passengers.

Taking a few involuntary steps backward, Claire watched in dry-mouthed dismay as the duo closed in on a young woman a few paces ahead of her, murmuring questions that Claire couldn't quite hear.

Alarm constricted her chest. They'd found her! Reporters from a television station had somehow discovered she'd taken this flight, and in a moment they'd pounce, ripping away her disguise for all the world to see. Grappling to hide her distress, she glanced around for another way out of the gate.

"Suzanne! Over here!" The deep, masculine yell resounded from somewhere beyond the gate. Out of her side view, Claire caught sight of a dark-haired man who towered head and shoulders above the crowd, moving with an easy gait in her general direction. "Suzanne, honey!"

As she turned toward the hoarse greeting out of sheer reflex, strong hands caught at her arms. "I missed you." And before she could do more than gape at the green-eyed stranger who gazed at her with jubilant welcome, he lifted her from the ground, whirled her around and crushed her against his muscled, T-shirted chest in a bear hug.

Nothing could have stunned Claire more. Except maybe a kiss, which he pressed against her temple. "John Peterson sent me," he whispered into her ear. "Claire Jones, right?"

She'd barely managed to nod at her assumed name when he set her back on her feet, hooked his arm around her shoulders and swept her forward, his body shielding her from the camera crew like a defensive linebacker protecting a quarterback.

"I don't think I'm going to let you go to any more of those seminars, honey," he declared in a booming jovial tone as he tugged her steadily away from the gate. "The boys missed you, too. Davey's barely eaten since you left. Must be my cooking."

He kept up a steady drone of nonsensical talk

as he hustled her along in the crook of his arm, forcing her into a half run to keep up with his long strides. She felt as if she'd been caught in an undertow and swept out to sea. Except this "undertow" surrounded her with warm, muscled brawn and the scent of a woodsy aftershave.

An irrelevant question flashed through her stunned female psyche. Had she ever been held this close by a man she didn't know? And had her blood ever hummed with such keen awareness of *any* man's touch? He was a stranger, a dark, virile stranger who held her as if she belonged to him....

Shaking herself out of a stupor, she realized she should ask for identification, although he *had* used her assumed name, which only Johnny had known. Still, she could take no chances. From the side of her mouth, she whispered, "Can I see some ID?"

"Pictures of the baby? Got 'em back just today." Reaching into the back pocket of his jeans, he pulled out his wallet and flipped it open. "Turned out great, didn't they?"

He held out a photo identification card that proclaimed him to be a licensed private investigator from Walker Investigative & Security Services. She nodded, and he slipped the wallet back into his pocket.

She hadn't caught his name.

Veering her away from the stream of travelers, he swept her down a quiet side corridor. He'd quit talking, but hadn't slowed his pace.

She was glad that Johnny had sent him, even

though she'd told him not to. He'd rescued her from the media. At least, he had so far....

They reached an elevator and he punched the Down button. His silence somehow revived her earlier tension and she pulled away from him, striving to find her voice. "What is your—?"

He laid a finger across her lips. Warmth washed through her from the brief contact. He shot a cautious glance both ways down the corridor. Though no one was in sight, his eyes returned to her with a stern warning to stay silent.

Anxiously she wondered if the reporters were following them or searching the airport with their cameras ready. How on earth had they discovered which flight she'd taken? And if the media had known about her flight, what about the authorities? Would they be searching for the woman who'd used identification with the name "Claire Jones" printed on it?

The steel doors slid open and her rescuer ushered her onto the empty elevator. She wrapped a nervous hand around the handrail for support as the doors closed. Her reflection in the stainless-steel walls startled her. The pale woman with tousled strawberry-blond curls, huge round sunglasses, cutoffs and a yellow T-shirt looked as much a stranger to her as the man standing beside her.

"What's your name?" she asked. "I didn't quite catch it from your ID."

He turned the full power of his gaze on her, and her pulse quickened. She didn't understand her reaction to him. Without his earlier smile, his face held no beauty—only a stark, rugged appeal comprised of lean angles, a strong jaw, a sun-bronzed complexion and eyes the color of a summer forest. A thin scar slanted across one high cheekbone, adding to the impression of street-wise toughness. His best claim to classic good looks was his raven hair, gleaming in careless waves that invited a woman's fingers to delve through their springy thickness....

"The name's Walker, ma'am." The low, whiskey-smooth reply could only be called deferential. Gone was the jubilant, husbandly tone. And gone was the warm welcome his gaze had held. He now regarded her with courteous, professional detachment. "I have a car waiting in a staff parking lot. We shouldn't have any trouble reaching it. I'll drive around for your luggage."

"I have no luggage."

He nodded curtly, betraying not a flicker of surprise.

She recognized him, then, with his readied stance, his tautly muscled physique, his impersonal gaze and protective air. She'd have known him anywhere. A bodyguard.

Only a bodyguard.

The old, stifling sense of solitude gripped her, more jarring than ever. It didn't matter who he was, how he looked, what he said...or how she had responded to his touch. He was a shadow, with no substance or meaning beyond his hired function. She'd lived with his kind long enough to know that.

She was, for all intents and purposes, alone. And as long as he was with her, she would remain alone, no matter how many people she might meet. He was a barrier, a human shield, between her and any potential enemy...or friend. She'd traveled across the country only to find herself once again in his isolating shadow.

Her anger stirred. She'd told Johnny not to send anyone. She'd warned him that no one could be trusted. This shadow-man who had spirited her away from the cameras could expose her just as easily. *Johnny! Oh, Johnny. Why didn't you listen to me?*

"What did John Peterson tell you about me?" She hadn't meant to ask the question; it had somehow slipped out before she could censor it.

He slanted her a glance. "You're a prize-winning poet who needs protection...right?"

She blinked. *A poet?* She remembered John swearing to keep her identity a secret, even to the man he hired to protect her. He'd obviously told him she was a poet. How creative!

"I've never met a poet laureate before," Walker remarked in a soft, admiring drawl. "I'm honored to serve you, ma'am. And I'll try my best to protect you from whatever crackpot is stalking you...and to keep the media off your back, as Mr. Peterson instructed."

She allowed herself a tentative smile. "I'm grateful to you for rescuing me back there."

"My pleasure." Something in his gaze set her blood to rushing.

Claire looked away and scolded herself. He'd uttered a common banality and her body had reacted as if he'd whispered an erotic suggestion. Perhaps the scent of freedom was acting as an aphrodisiac, turning her thoughts to the sensual.

And why wouldn't her thoughts turn to the sensual? She'd had no lover other than Preston—they'd been engaged forever, it seemed—and it had been months since they'd been alone together. He'd kept a busy schedule. After seeing those photos of him with other women, she realized that she had been the only one to remain faithful. A desperate restlessness had kept her awake at nights. She'd felt as if life were passing her by.

It had been. And now she would make up for lost time.

The elevator doors opened and Walker escorted her out into a maze of concrete corridors. Her spirits had risen immeasurably. He hadn't a clue as to her real identity. She would ride out of this airport with him and—assuming the media was not in hot pursuit—direct him to a hotel. She'd dismiss him then. His job would be done. By the time the news broke of Valentina's disappearance and Walker connected her with John Peterson, she'd be long gone.

And, amazingly, free!

She found herself smiling as she followed Walker out to a parking garage. When he gestured toward a midsize gray sedan, she was surprised for the briefest moment that the car was not a limousine. Not that she was displeased. She liked the idea of riding in something other than a limo. Marveling over that simple difference, she stopped near the sedan's back door.

Walker stopped near the front door.

Claire stared at him blankly.

"Excuse me, ma'am," he said in his deep, low voice that somehow warmed her insides, "if those reporters happen to see us driving away, they might wonder why my, uh, *wife* is sitting alone in the back seat."

Although he'd spoken with all the deferential courtesy one expected of one's bodyguard, Claire swore she saw a gleam of humor in his gaze. But it was quickly gone, and he waited with stoic patience for her reply. He meant, of course, for her to sit in the front seat instead of her usual place in the back.

A realization dawned on her then with an uplifting rush. This was one of those things that had suddenly changed. She could sit in the front beside the driver, *and no one would care!* And that was just the beginning. She could do all the things she'd always wanted to do; things her uncle, advisors, fiancé and peers would have frowned at. Yes, she thought. Yes!

She would be...an average "Jane Doe." Or rather, "Claire Jones." She'd blend in with the common people—wear, say and do the things they did. And no one would give her a second glance, unless it was simply because she was doing something outrageous. Even then, they wouldn't recognize her.

A little spurt of happiness bubbled up from her heart. "You're absolutely right," she told her new bodyguard-driver-pseudo-husband. "The front it'll be." She couldn't stop herself from beaming at him.

Her smile seemed to take him aback.

Why?

There I go again, she scolded herself. Craving approval. Needing a quick fix of it...and from a temporary bodyguard, no less. A very temporary bodyguard. Good Lord, she'd even catered to her servants' likes and dislikes, she realized—classical music in the limo to please her driver, French cuisine for dinner to please her chef, starch in her blouses to please her laundress. No more, she swore. She would dedicate herself to discovering her own tastes and preferences—to liberating the real Claire—and to hell with anyone who didn't like her.

Yeah. That was the spirit.

Before climbing into the car, she stopped directly in front of the dark, unreadable man who held the door for her. "I'd like you to drive me to a downtown hotel, please."

"A downtown hotel?" He frowned. "John Peterson had me rent a cabin for you in the mountains."

Surprised, she considered the idea for a moment, then decided against it. She'd had enough of isolation. She wanted to be an anonymous face in a lively crowd. "No, I'd rather go to a hotel."

"Any kind of crowd can pose a danger to you, Ms. Jones."

"Would you rather I take an airport limo? I wouldn't mind. Really."

He compressed his lips briefly, then murmured, "I'd be pleased to drive you anywhere you want to go."

"Thank you. Cancel the cabin, then. And once we're out of this airport, I'm going to turn on the radio and play some rock and roll. Hard rock. Loud." She climbed into the front seat and added, "With all the windows down."

He quirked one brow as he closed her door. "Yes, ma'am."

Within moments they were leaving the airport behind, motoring along Interstate 85, the electric guitar music blaring, their hair whipping about in the wind from the open windows.

Tyce couldn't remember seeing anyone look quite so happy. Her fingers drummed on the armrest in time to the beat as she gazed around in bright interest at the Atlanta skyline.

He was getting used to her smile now. The first time she'd smiled at him—really smiled—he'd felt as if the breath had been knocked out of him. She was just too damn beautiful to go around smiling like that, even with those huge sunglasses on, especially if she didn't want to be noticed.

She'd be noticed, all right. He hadn't been able to stop "noticing" her since he'd found her in the airport, looking alone and lost…and elegantly regal despite the cutoffs, T-shirt and tangled mop of curls. Maybe it was the way she held herself, or the grace of her movements. Whatever it was, she'd stand out in any crowd, especially if she smiled.

He supposed he might be more sensitive to it than others. That one covert glance at her all those years ago through the telescopic lens had profoundly marked him. Without ever meaning to, he'd taken her with him into his nighttime fantasies; borrowed her face and body for his own private use.

Now when he looked at her, sitting beside him in person, a real woman suddenly attached to the face and body of his imaginary lover, an occasional shock went through him. He didn't know this woman at all; didn't *want* to know her. But his body felt as if he had.

He'd been hoping she'd go for the mountain cabin suggestion. He'd come up with the idea shortly after sweeping her into his arms. He could rent one with a quick phone call.

Just as easily—with one quick phone call—she could discover his lies. Her cousin, John Peterson, hadn't hired him, of course, nor had he rented her a cabin. Tyce was banking on her statement to Johnny that she wouldn't call him for a month out of fear that the call might be traced. Her fear was certainly legitimate. But if she changed her mind and called, Tyce's game would be up.

Until then, she was his.

His *responsibility*, he amended.

He'd been hired by her uncle to find her and report on her activities.

It somewhat bothered Tyce that Edgar Richmond hadn't included protection in the agreement. Protecting his niece had not been part of Edgar's instructions. But how could Tyce possibly keep her under surveillance without also protecting her?

He just couldn't.

Hence, the bodyguard act. He could protect her *and* keep her under surveillance this way.

A crowd would make both of those tasks difficult. A cabin in the mountains seemed the perfect solution. He'd have to find a way to get her there, whether she liked it or not. After cruising the Mediterranean and skiing in the Swiss Alps, Her Highness might consider an Appalachian mountain view akin to a jail cell.

Too bad.

Impatiently he checked his rearview mirror. Fred should be coming up behind them anytime now. Tyce hoped Fred and his other operatives would do a better job at tailing than they had with the video camera and microphone ruse at the airport. They'd let him slip away with her too easily.

C'mon, Fred. Tail us, damn it. A little more anxiety might change her mind about going to a downtown hotel.

"Hey, is that a Burger World?" cried his passenger, pointing toward the exit ramp. "It is! Oh, Walker, let's go. Do you know how long it's been since I've had a Whomper?" Uncertainty clouded her face. "They still make them, don't they?"

"Well, yeah."

"Great! Let's go. And…we'll get it from the drive-thru window." She said it as if that aspect of the experience was some great adventure.

He shrugged to himself. Apparently her limousines hadn't pulled up to drive-thru windows very often. With one last glance in his rearview mirror, he veered off the expressway toward Burger World. He hoped Fred had noticed the move…*if* Fred was even back there.

She studied the drive-thru menu with open delight, then asked if she could do the ordering. "I've never ordered through one of these speakers before. The few times we've stopped, my drivers always did the ordering."

He hoped she wouldn't say things like that to just anybody. They'd be bound to wonder who she was.

She leaned innocently across him to call her order into the loudspeaker, an activity she did with gusto. Her nearness afforded him another whiff of her delicate roselike scent, which he'd noticed when he'd hugged her at the airport. It had surprised him, the sweet simplicity of her fragrance. He'd expected something more opulent from the Perfume Princess. The scent of roses, subtle though it was, had mingled with her warmth to fill his head during their embrace. She'd felt incredibly good in his arms—slender, vibrant and much too kissable.

"What'll *you* have, Walker?" She was very near him again, her face only inches from his.

"Nothing for me."

"Oh, *please* have something." Although he couldn't see her eyes through her sunglasses, which she hadn't yet removed for even a moment, she peered at him with such childlike expectation that he couldn't refuse her.

"Coffee."

She twisted her mouth in wry disapproval and tossed her head, making her sunset-colored curls dance, but shouted his order into the loudspeaker, anyway. She insisted on paying for his as well as hers.

When she opened her purse, his attention was immediately snagged by her cash—small bundles of denominations including hundreds and fifties, haphazardly crammed into her purse as if she'd just knocked off a bank.

Carefully she extricated dollar bills and counted them out with patient care. She probably hadn't handled cash very often, he realized. Everything she wanted would have been charged, he guessed, or paid for by a personal protection agent. She couldn't, of course, use her credit cards for this trip. They'd give away her identity and leave too easy a trail to follow.

But all that cash made her a target for petty thieves. She could get mugged for it.

"You shouldn't be carrying around that much cash," he admonished when she'd been handed the drinks and food.

Her eyes met his in surprise. "But I'll need it. My credit cards are, uh, were stolen."

"A small amount of cash is fine, but you're carrying too much, and it's too visible. Why don't we stop at a bank and get traveler's checks?" The moment he'd suggested it, he knew she'd refuse. She'd be forced to buy and sign them with her fraudulent name.

She bit her full bottom lip and turned her attention to her milk shake, which she carefully set down in the dashboard cup holder. "I, uh, prefer using cash."

"Then put some of it in your—" He broke off abruptly. She couldn't very well put any in her suitcase since she didn't *have* one.

Good Lord, she did indeed need his protection.

Unperturbed, she savored her burger, fries and chocolate milk shake while he drove. Tyce searched his rearview mirror for sight of Fred. He hoped he'd show up soon. He had a sneaking suspicion that Valentina planned to fire him the moment they reached a hotel. From her phone conversation with her cousin, he knew she hadn't wanted a driver or a bodyguard.

He simply had to supply her with the right motivation to want one. *Where the hell are you, Fred?*

While supposedly driving her to a hotel, Tyce gave his employee time to find them by taking his passenger on a tour of Atlanta, pointing out the stadium built for the Olympics, the capitol's golden dome, the architecturally unique skyscrapers and towers. She nodded in appreciation over each sight, but the one that drew her excitement wasn't on his tour.

He'd turned off onto a side street and she spotted a discount variety store. "Look—a Value Village!" More to herself than to him, she murmured, "Nanny used to shop at those." After a ponderous moment, she decided, "I'd like to shop at Value Village for a while, if you don't mind."

He *did* mind. It was too public of a place. But he let her go in, anyway. He couldn't very well stop her.

When an elderly employee greeted her at the door with a shopping cart—a routine courtesy extended at every Value Village—she profusely thanked him, exclaiming, "A cart! What a wonderful idea."

Tyce supposed the shops in Rodeo Drive didn't have shopping carts. He trailed her at a discreet distance, watching as she flitted from aisle to aisle, exploring. He took the opportunity to call Fred on his cell phone. Fred, it seemed, was having car trouble. This little shopping break would give him time to catch up with them.

Just as he slipped his cell phone back into his pocket, Valentina caught sight of him following her down the Women's Accessories aisle, and stopped with a horrified look on her face. "You're following me."

He sauntered up to her, unperturbed. "Yes, ma'am."

"Why?"

"Mr. Peterson hired me to watch out for you, remember?"

She compressed her lips and raised her chin, her delicate nostrils flaring. She did indeed look like a miffed princess. All she said, however, was, "If you must follow me, then at least walk with me." In a softer, more hesitant tone, she added, "Pretend we're friends."

He hesitated. *Pretend we're friends.* He wasn't sure he knew how to do that. He couldn't remember the last time he'd *had* a friend.

Or rather, he didn't *want* to remember the last time he'd had what he considered a friend—fourteen years ago. He'd never allow himself another. He'd just as soon lay open his veins and let the blood flow than open his heart that way.

But she'd only asked him to pretend.

She seemed to take his cooperation for granted as she turned her attention to the shelves around them. Pulling down a large-brimmed straw hat, she held up a smaller white sun hat in her other hand. "Which one of these looks better?" She tried on each of them.

He liked her better with her hair dancing freely about her face, but he nodded toward the straw hat. Her sunny smile returned, full force, and she filled a shopping cart with clothes, cosmetics, shoes and luggage. "I didn't bring much with me," she explained. "I'll need a few things."

Blithely she moved on to the lingerie department. He couldn't help noticing the items she chose—sheer nighties, lacy bikini panties, satiny bras. Sexy, see-through things that were having an uncomfortable effect on him. He couldn't help picturing how she'd look in every wicked little piece. And how creative he could get, taking it off of her...

He was thoroughly relieved when she headed for the checkout counter. Another adventure for her—setting each item on the rotating belt and watching the clerk ring up her purchases on the cash register.

He had to admit, this princess puzzled him. She had to be accustomed to only the most expensive merchandise from world-class designers, yet here she was, shopping happily at Value Village. It had to be the novelty of it. He could see Hattie's headlines now: The Perfume Princess Goes Slumming.

Uneasiness glanced through him. The role of bodyguard that he'd lightly assumed as a ruse now weighed heavily on his shoulders. He couldn't let her get hurt. He needed to get her out of here, out of the public's eye, before she *was* recognized. Anytime now, the news of her running away was bound to break.

When she'd paid for her purchases, Tyce took hold of her elbow and steered her to the car. He opened her door, but before she settled in, she touched his shoulder and said in a quiet, shy way, "Thank you, Walker, for bringing me here and shopping with me. I know it was probably a bore for you, but I...I really did appreciate the company."

She meant it, he knew. Her gratitude was heart-felt. Which bothered the hell out of him.

She distracted him then with a soft smile that curved her lips—smooth, full, naturally rosy lips. He wondered what they'd taste like. And if her eyes, still concealed behind her sunglasses, could possibly pack the same punch to a man's gut. He vaguely remembered blue eyes from her photos. He suddenly wanted to see them for himself, those eyes she'd kept hidden from him.

She slid into the front seat of his car.

He slammed her door without replying to her thank-you or returning her smile. Why the hell should she be grateful to him? It was his job, as far as she knew, to take her wherever she wanted to go and to watch over her. She shouldn't care whether he'd been bored or not. She shouldn't "appreciate his company." She shouldn't be that transparently vulnerable.

With a sudden urge to toughen her up, to force her to lie—to make sure she *could* lie—he asked as he started up the car, "So what kind of poetry do you write, Ms. Jones?"

She glanced at him, obviously taken aback. "What kind? Oh…the kind that rhymes." After another moment, she ventured, "And sometimes the kind that doesn't." Worrying her bottom lip with her teeth, she asked, "Do you read poetry?"

"Not really. But I wouldn't mind stopping at a bookstore and picking up one of your volumes. Having you autograph it for me."

The alarm on her face was much too obvious,

even with her eyes veiled by those damn sunglasses. "No, I'm sorry, we don't have time to stop at a bookstore. I have to get settled into a hotel as soon as possible."

"Recite one of your poems for me, then."

She opened her mouth, but no words came out.

He narrowed his gaze and watched her squirm. She wasn't a very good liar. He couldn't resist pushing her a little further. "You can't recite even *a few lines* from one of your poems?"

The silence between them thickened.

Claire noticed the inexplicably stern expression on his face and felt as if she were failing some test. But he had no right to test her! He was only a bodyguard. She didn't need his approval. She should simply order him to leave her alone.

But she hated to ruin the mood of her first day of freedom. And though no one in the world knew it, she *had* scribbled a few lines of verse that could be considered a poem. She'd written it in one of her darkest fits of boredom.

"Okay," she relented. "But only a few lines."

His stern expression dissolved into something that resembled surprise.

She herself was somewhat surprised. As Valentina Richmond, she never would have shared these lines with a living soul. They might have found their way into a tabloid and embarrassed the heck out of her. But as Claire Jones, she didn't have to worry about things like that. Taking a deep breath, she announced, "I call this one, 'Stagnation.'"

"Ah," he said. "A love poem."

She flashed him an impish grin. "How did you guess?"

"Let's hear it."

Enjoying herself immensely, she proclaimed, "'I don't want to exist, I want to live.'" She paused, and he nodded his encouragement to continue. Heartened, she went on,

"'I don't want to take, I want to give.
I don't want to talk, I want to yell.
I don't want to say heck, I want to say hell!'"

Her voice had risen, and she found herself saying the words with feeling; punctuating each line with her fist.

"'Don't want to argue, I want to fight.
Don't want to hold on, I want to squeeze tight.
Don't want a dime, I want a buck!
Don't want a hug, I want a—'"

She paused, her fist still in the air, and met his glance. With a quirky smile, she finished, "'kiss for good luck.'"

Abject silence followed.

She lowered her fist to her lap.

Her one-man audience didn't applaud. He didn't make a sound. He'd returned his gaze to the road and seemed to be poking his tongue against the inside of his cheek. Finally he lifted a brow. "*That* won you the Poet Laureate?"

"No, I'm saving *this* literary gem for my next volume."

And then he laughed—a short, surprised bark of masculine laughter that turned her heart over.

"Want to hear it again?" she teased.

"No, once is plenty. Every word will remain forever etched in my memory."

"Good. You can say it with me, then."

"No, really. Rock and roll might be good now. Real loud. With all the windows down."

Feeling absurdly happy as their gazes connected, she turned on the radio and lowered the windows. "I know that poem was bad, Walker," she shouted above the roar of the wind. "But I *want* to be bad. I've been good for too darned long. For too *damn* long," she corrected with a self-satisfied grin.

His smile wavered a bit, and he shouted, "What do you mean, you want to be 'bad'?"

"Naughty. Wicked. Completely *inappropriate*."

He looked uncomfortable with the confidence.

She didn't care. She flung her arms wide, as if she were flying in the roaring wind, and went on with exuberance. "I'm going to sow my wild oats!"

He didn't reply.

"I might go to a bar tonight and dance like a maniac. And get drunk, if I feel like it. Who knows? I might meet someone. I might even... start smoking."

"Smoking!"

"Yes! Oh, yes," she decided, clasping her hands together. "It would be perfect. Pull over at the next convenience store, Walker. I want a pack of cigarettes."

"Absolutely not."

"I beg your pardon?"

"It's a hard habit to break. Don't start."

"I don't mean to hurt your feelings, but it's really none of your business whether I—"

"I'm supposed to protect you, right?"

"Well, I suppose."

"Smoking can kill you, just like a psychotic gunman can. You're not going to do it on my watch. Besides, I don't allow smoking in my car."

"But I—"

"I think we're being followed." His attention was snared by his rearview mirror, his expression suddenly grim.

"Followed?" She frowned as he studied the traffic behind them through his mirrors.

"That blue van back there. I saw it when we left Value Village, and now it's two cars behind us."

She turned around in her seat and spotted the van in the traffic behind them. Her heart dropped. She'd thought they'd left the media back at the airport.

"Hold on," instructed Walker. "We're going to lose 'em."

As they pulled up even with an exit ramp, he cut the wheel sharply, crossed two lanes of honking traffic and drove over concrete ridges onto the ramp.

And with an awful squeal of tires and blaring of horns, the blue van swerved in the exact same path, up the exit ramp, to follow them.

3

HE SHOVED HER down onto the bench seat, then grabbed the wheel with both hands, forcing it into a hard turn. The car leaped and lurched, slinging Claire halfway to the floor and dislodging the sunglasses from her face. She caught hold of Walker's leg, pulled herself up and clung to him. His iron-strong thigh muscles flexed beneath her hands as he worked the accelerator and brake.

The chase was on.

Claire's heart hammered with fear as her mind sprang from one possibility to the next. Paparazzi? Undercover law enforcement of some kind? Her crazy stalker? Would she be assaulted with cameras or arrest warrants or bullets?

Anxious to see, she tried to raise her head. Walker pressed it back down, lodging her face against his lap. "Stay down," he ordered gruffly, lifting his hand from her hair where it had briefly lingered, "until I'm sure I've lost them."

"Them? How many of them are there in the van?" she cried against the rough denim of his jeans, wishing he'd kept his hand on her head. She'd felt oddly safe with him touching her.

"At least two."

Then it probably wasn't the stalker. "Do they look like paparazzi?"

"Can't tell."

Anger diluted her fear. Damn them! Damn whoever was following her. She had the right to her privacy, her freedom. Men had died on battlefields for those rights.

Walker eased off the accelerator, made a few turns and, after an eternity, pulled to a stop.

Claire realized she was lying in his lap, facedown. Thank goodness, at least, that he couldn't see her face. Her sunglasses had fallen off. He might have recognized her. In that instant, she realized she didn't want to dodge these unknown pursuers alone. She needed Walker, at least for the time being. If he were to guess her real identity, though, she'd have to run from him, too. The media offered big bucks for stories about her. He could sell her out with one quick call.

"You okay?" he asked in that sultry gruff voice of his.

"I'm fine." Snatching her sunglasses from the floorboard, she sat up, turning to face him only when the large tortoiseshell frames were securely in place. She found him studying her with veiled eyes, his dark, rugged face unreadable. "How could anyone have found me?" she asked, dismayed at the slight tremor in her voice. "There weren't any cars following us from the airport."

"Sometimes tails are hard to spot."

"There was no one tailing us," she insisted.

Her absolute certainty surprised Tyce. She'd

been paying closer attention than he'd thought. No one *had* followed them from the airport.

"How dare they?" she fumed. "This is my *life* they're trying so hard to ruin. I'll be damned if I'll let them." She reached into the back seat and grabbed a few packages of newly purchased items. "Drive to the far back corner of this parking lot," she ordered tersely, "over there between that Dumpster and those trees."

Curious at her request and surprised by her anger when he'd been expecting only anxiety, Tyce silently guided the sedan across the vacant lot of a boarded-up grocery store. Was she angry *at him?* Had she realized that he'd hired the van to follow them? He didn't see how she could have known.

He parked behind the oak-shaded Dumpster. She slung open her door and hopped out, her packages under her arm and her purse in her hand. Tyce sprang out from his side and bounded around to her, sure she intended to run.

He stopped in bewilderment.

She had deposited all of her belongings on the hood of his car and bent to unbuckle her sandals. As he watched, she stepped out of the strappy littleshoes and pitched them into the Dumpster. Her slender, lightly tanned feet were now bare... and she was struggling to unclasp the gold bracelet from her wrist.

"What the hell are you doing?" he demanded.

"Bugs," she said with conviction, her bright curls falling across her sunglasses as she worked at the clasp of her bracelet. "Electronic bugs. There's probably one or two on me."

"You think someone's trying to *listen* to us?"

"Not the kind of bug that records voices—the tracking kind. There's no other way they could have known where I was. Someone must have stuck a tracking device on me...at one of the airports, maybe. Or in the plane itself. Or maybe even before I left home." The bracelet came loose from her wrist. Without a moment's hesitation, she threw the gleaming gold filigree over the top of the huge Dumpster.

"Are you planning to throw away everything you brought with you?" he asked incredulously.

"Everything except my cash. They wouldn't have bugged that, would they? I mean, I could have spent it anywhere. The device has to be on *me* somewhere. I have to get rid of it and hit the road before they circle back." Panic edged her voice and she glanced wildly around. "They'll be coming any minute, I'm sure." She reached up to remove the golden hoops from her ears.

"Wait." He caught her hand to stop her from removing her earrings. He couldn't stand watching her throw away her things when the only one in hot pursuit had been Fred. "You don't have to throw everything away. I'd know an electronic tagging device if I found it. All I have to do is look."

"Are you sure, Walker? Absolutely, positively, sure you wouldn't miss any? I could easily throw everything I'm wearing away and put on the clothes I just bought."

"You're planning to throw your clothes away, too? Here and now?" He tried hard to ignore the mental image she'd conjured up.

"Of course! My personal maid might have—I mean, *anyone* might have bugged my clothes the night before I left. I didn't think anyone knew what I'd be wearing, but I could have been wrong. I *had* set them aside the night before…"

"Oh. Oh, yeah…I see what you mean." Her logic was getting the best of him. Or maybe it was the idea of conducting an intimate body search….

"We have to check everything, Walker. Everything."

His breathing had somehow gone shallow. "Better safe than sorry."

She handed him her earrings, and he handed them back to her. "These are too small and fine to hide a tag," he said. "You'd spot it immediately."

"Check my purse." She grabbed handfuls of her cash and tossed the bundles onto the front seat of the car, then held the comb, lipstick and other sundries in her cupped hands. Cautiously he ran his hands over the large, carpetbag-style handbag, both inside and out. She then gave him the rest of her purse's contents to inspect, which he did with great care. "No tags here."

"It has to be in my clothes, then."

He had to make at least one attempt to talk her out of it. "There *are* some new, highly sophisticated devices that could be hidden in clothing, but very few people have access to that type of…of…"

To his amazement, she pulled her T-shirt over her head and handed it to him, standing there between his car, the Dumpster and the shady oaks with her arms crossed over her lacy white bra. He really hadn't thought she'd do it. "Hurry, Walker. That van will be coming back for us."

Trying his best not to stare at her, he ran the cottony T-shirt through his fingers, conscious of her body warmth and delicate rose scent that clung to the yellow fabric…and of the woman dressed in only a bra, short cutoffs and sunglasses.

"Do you feel anything?" she asked in an anxious whisper.

Hell, yeah, he felt something. "No," he managed to say. "No tags."

She took the T-shirt from him and held it closely in front of her, hiding the lush curves that rose above the white lace. "It has to be here somewhere, Walker. It has to be. There's no other way they could have found me."

"Do you want me to…keep looking?"

She nodded.

He obliged. Who was he to say for positively sure that no one had tagged her before she left home? If they had, her life itself could be in danger. He had a duty to uphold. A duty. He turned her around, his hands momentarily savoring her silken bare shoulders and the bouncy curls brushing them. He proceeded to inspect the back clasp of her bra, running his fingers along the strap, sincerely trying to concentrate on his search for an electronic microtag rather than the warm, tender skin against the backs of his fingers. He hadn't imagined her skin to be quite this soft. He hadn't imagined that touching her would get to him quite this much...

Why should it? She wasn't naked—she was wearing considerably more than most women would on a public beach. He wasn't an inexperienced kid—he'd had his share of beautiful women. But something about the sight and feel of this one turned his thoughts to rumpled beds and night-long lovemaking.

She was a billionaire celebrity, damn it. One of the jet set. American royalty. He was a fool to even touch her.

More brusquely than he intended, he turned her around to face him. She held the doffed T-shirt clasped to her chest. Her face, though half concealed by sunglasses, had flushed to a rosy red.

"Think of me as a doctor," he suggested.

She swallowed, nodded and lowered the T-shirt enough for him to continue his inspection.

Clenching his back teeth, he ran his fingertips around the elastic lower edge of her bra, feeling nothing but womanly warmth and softness and the pounding of her heart. Before he could stop himself, he'd moved his hands across the full, warm, satiny cups. Rigid peaks rose up beneath his palms. His body hardened in tight, demanding response, and he fought the desire to rub those diamond-hard crests.

"Find anything?" she breathed.

"Uh-uh."

"Keep searching." The moment he'd removed his hands from her breasts, she slipped back into her T-shirt. Her nipples were still visible, poking through the thin cotton. Heat coiled and writhed inside him like a snake about to strike.

Struggling to contain it, he bent his attention to her cutoffs, inspecting the pockets, the rivets and the waistband, inside and out. Her waist was so narrow, he discovered, and her abdomen so flat, that her skin barely touched the waistband at all. Plenty of room for a man to slip his hand inside. Sucking in a cooling draft of air through his nostrils, he withdrew from that temptation, only to confront the curvaceous exterior.

He had a job to do—a tough job—and he'd see it through or die trying. *Times like these tried men's souls...*

After checking her back pockets, he smoothed his hands over the pleasing mounds of her backside, going down on his knees to be thorough. Though his breathing had grown strained, he persevered, feeling his way around to her slender hips, which fit nicely between his hands. Hips made for a man to hold on to as he thrust himself inside her...

"Anything yet?"

"Not so far," he reported in a voice far too hoarse.

"Maybe…the zipper?" Her whisper sounded just as husky as his.

His hands shook, his blood rushed. He unzipped her shorts and felt his way along both edges of the jagged tracks.

"Hurry, Walker, before they find us."

He couldn't quite force the "Yes, ma'am" from his throat. She wore sheer white bikini panties— silky against the backs of his knuckles—and near the bottom of the open zipper glimmered golden-blond curls, barely visible beneath the fine lace.

He expelled his breath in a hard, jittery rush and forced himself to zip her back up. He was too damn close to forgetting that they were in a public place, shielded only by his car, a grove of trees and a Dumpster. Too close to forgetting who she was and why they were there. He wanted to press his face against the lace, peel it off her, kiss his way to where he wanted to be. Make fast, hard love to her, heiress or not.

He forced himself to his feet, hot and dizzy with wanting her. Had she been turned on, he wondered, or was he just imagining the sexuality radiating like heat waves between them? He realized then, as his gaze reached her face, that she was still wearing her sunglasses.

"Your glasses," he rasped. "Give 'em to me."

Her lips parted, her color deepened. "You…you think the tag might be on my glasses?"

"Might be. I'd better check."

She moved a step back from him. "Can't you just check while they're *on* me?"

He could, of course. He'd just checked her bra and shorts while they were very much "on her." But he heard himself saying in a smooth, authoritative tone, "Glasses are different than clothes. Most electronic tags can be felt on fabric much easier than on metal or glass." It wasn't necessarily true, but she wouldn't know that.

Dismay crossed her face. She wanted to refuse.

He wanted to force the issue. He wanted to see her eyes. To read them. "If there *is* a tag on those sunglasses," he warned, "that blue van should be zeroing in on us any moment."

With a little cry, she turned her slender back to him, whipped off her glasses and held them out. "My eyes are overly sensitive to the sun," she explained, pressing her free hand over the entire top half of her face. "From medication I'm taking."

Tyce's lips tightened as he took the glasses. He felt as if she were teasing him, holding out on him, showing him just so much of her and no more. She'd allowed him to slip his hand in her shorts, but wouldn't let him see her eyes!

He realized, of course, that she was afraid he'd recognize her. And if he were thinking straight, he'd be glad of her determination to stay shielded. She'd be easier to protect if no one recognized her. Problem was, he *wasn't* thinking straight. He wanted to see her eyes…up close and personal.

Grudgingly he inspected the expensive sunglasses. He almost hoped there would be a tag on them, just to ease his conscience. Chances had been slim that she'd been tagged, and he'd known it before he'd started his body search. But why should he feel guilty? Any red-blooded man would have complied with her wishes. Maybe that's what bothered him. She was too naive to be out in the world alone. Too trusting of a man she didn't know.

With a self-deprecating smirk, he grimaced. What was he thinking? She was a beautiful woman who'd grown up among the power players in a wickedly political world. She couldn't possibly be as naive as she seemed. He wasn't sure why she had run away, though he guessed she was angry over her fiancé's infidelity and was now determined to "sow her wild oats," as she'd put it. Sweet revenge. Or maybe she was involved in some political intrigue. Whatever the reason for her covert flight, this "princess" was no babe in the woods, no matter how trusting she seemed to be.

She wouldn't, after all, let him see her face. Which meant she didn't really trust him worth a damn.

"Here," he muttered, placing the sunglasses in her outstretched hand. "They're clean."

As she put the sunglasses back on, he leaned into the car and pulled from his glove compartment a small kit, which he slipped into his jeans' pocket. And while she busied herself packing her possessions into the back seat, he opened the kit, withdrew a microdot electronic tracking device, and attached it to her purse. Just in case she tried to give him the slip.

"If there weren't any electronic devices on me," she pondered, nestled in the passenger seat once more as he settled behind the wheel, "then how did that blue van find us?"

"The device was probably on the bracelet or sandals you pitched in the Dumpster."

"Hmm. Too bad we don't have the time to find them and see."

"Yeah. Too bad." He started up the car.

She frowned, shivered and glanced both ways down the quiet side street. "At least we've lost the van for now. We'd better get far away from here, and quick. I'd wanted to spend some time in Atlanta, but I think it might be risky." After a moment she decided. "Head south."

"South? What about that cabin up north that I mentioned earlier?"

"I'd rather visit Florida. Panama City Beach, I think."

"Panama City!" He'd figured her more for the Greek Isles or South of France type. "There's bound to be capacity crowds this time of year— either families or hell-raising partygoers."

"Sounds perfect." She smiled and leaned her head back against the seat, her rosy-blond curls cascading like a waterfall, her slender throat alluringly exposed.

A sudden impulse possessed him—to press a kiss against her throat, just beneath the tender underside of her jaw; to taste the skin that had felt like heaven beneath his hands. Shifting uncomfortably in his seat, he realized this was going to be one long drive—much longer than the six hours it would actually take to get to Florida.

"I'm in the mood for crowds, Walker." Her voice grew soft and dreamy. "Lots of frolicking vacationers on the beaches...in the bars...on the miracle strip...."

Tyce scowled and gripped the wheel harder. The chase hadn't worried her as much as he'd hoped. She still wanted to be around crowds. He certainly couldn't *force* her up to that mountain cabin. There went his hopes of getting her alone.

Maybe it was better this way, he grudgingly mused. In his present state of mind—and body— he'd pose more of a danger to her than the crowds would.

THEY DROVE in tense silence. The afternoon gradually gave way to evening and the expressway to a two-lane country road. Darkness descended. Hazy country moonlight replaced the glare of urban streetlights.

As she rested her head against the seat and closed her eyes, Claire kept her sunglasses on. She felt vulnerable at the moment. Intensely vulnerable. Despite the fact that she didn't know the man at all, Walker's body search had left her so aroused she'd barely been able to walk to the car. Maybe it had been the danger of the moment, knowing her enemies were actively hunting her, or her own long-repressed desire to be naughty. Maybe it had been the sheer sexual appeal of a man as solidly masculine as Walker. Whatever the reason, she'd never before felt as wanton as she had while his hands and eyes had moved over her.

Even now, her body simmered with sensual longing. She wanted him to reach across the seat and stroke her with those strong, bronzed hands; feel her breasts, rouse her nipples to that exquisite sensitivity that left her aching for more. She'd unzip her shorts, welcome his hand inside...she'd seek out the hardness she hoped to find behind his zipper—

That thought brought her up sharp. Had he been aroused? If so, he hadn't shown it. He'd been positively wooden-faced the entire time he inspected her, doing nothing more than what she'd asked. Maybe she wasn't his type. When it came to sex, she hadn't been her own fiancé's type, it seemed. He'd sought out other woman to satisfy his sexual needs when he could have been with her.

What was she lacking in the sexuality department?

She'd been called beautiful by the press—an exaggeration, she knew, but people seemed to believe it. In fact, they believed it too much. She knew she didn't live up to the glamorous image the media had created for Valentina Richmond.

When it came down to reality—to just plain

Claire—would all men find her lacking? A troubling question. Very troubling.

Doubts about her sexual appeal should, by all rights, have doused the inner fire Walker had lit with his intimate touches and veiled eyes. But erotic images of things he could do to her...and she to him...kept her blood on a low simmer for hours.

Walker, meanwhile, kept his eyes on the road.

"Walker," she said as they drew closer to their destination in the small hours of the night, "are you married?" She'd hit upon this possibility with a good measure of relief. Not only would she then understand his lack of sexual interest in her, but she'd respect him all the more for it.

"No."

She wasn't sure if she should be glad or insulted. "Are you...in love?"

He looked at her as if he might tell her to mind her own business. After a moment, though, he surprised her by answering, "I thought I was, once."

Maybe that was it—he was recently heartbroken. "How long ago?"

"Many years." He smiled, but without humor. "I was eighteen. Her daddy disapproved."

"So you stopped seeing her?"

"I wasn't that gallant. He had the hell beat out of me, just to get his point across."

A cry escaped her. "How terrible! Was he held liable for it?"

"He was old money. I was a kid from the

streets." He slanted her a glance through the moonlit darkness. "What do you think?"

His cynicism took her by surprise. There did indeed seem to be some unresolved emotional issues here, but not quite the kind she'd imagined. "What did his daughter do?"

He shrugged, his intensity gone as quickly as it had come. "Told me to quit coming around. Found herself a more suitable boyfriend." After a reflective silence, he added softly, "I'm no aristocrat, Princess."

Her body went stiff. "*What* did you call me?"

He winced, as if regretting a slipup.

"Did you call me...'Princess'?" She stared at him, her heart now pounding with something more than desire. She'd been called "Princess" by the paparazzi and the general public for as long as she could remember. Did he know who she was?

"If I offended you, I'm sorry," he said. "I meant it only as a...a figure of speech. A casual endearment. You know, like 'Sweetheart' or...or 'Sugar.'" He sounded as if he were floundering. "I know that none of those is politically correct, but I have a bad habit of saying them anyway when I'm talking to a...a woman like you."

"Like me?" Her insecurities rose up to taunt her. Perhaps he saw her as haughty or spoiled. Maybe that's why he'd called her princess. She couldn't help the frosty tone as she inquired, "Like me, in what way?"

He took a moment to reply. "Poised. Elegant."

He studied the road for a good long while, then said in a curiously gruff whisper, "Beautiful."

Something inside her leaped, warmed and glowed. How foolish of her, to take a compliment so to heart. She'd practically forced him into flattering her.

His gaze was a silent, serious request for forgiveness. "I meant no disrespect. My apologies...ma'am."

Bothered by her growing attraction to this perfect stranger, she could only hope she was justified in giving him the benefit of her doubt. He probably *had* tossed out the word "princess" in a casual, offhanded way. "Please," she whispered, "call me Claire."

"Claire."

The soft, reverent way he said her name filled her with an almost painful warmth. "The only time I want you to call me by one of your 'casual endearments,'" she said, her own voice hushed and somber, "is if you mean it."

And it was there again between them, intensified by their stares—the oddly intimate silence that left her feeling so vulnerable.

THE DREAM CAME to him with such vivid horror that he woke with a start, his muscles clenched and his breathing rapid. It took a moment to realize where he was—on the living room sofa bed of the condo they'd rented. He shut his eyes in the darkness and willed his heart to stop racing.

He hadn't dreamed of the fight in years. He

supposed he had now because he'd spoken of it. He rarely did. Why had he told her? At least he hadn't told her all of it. Maybe that was why the untold parts had replayed in his dream.

He hadn't been alone that night fourteen years ago when his girlfriend's father had sent thugs to work him over. He'd been with a friend—a good friend who had grown up with him on the mean Los Angeles streets. They'd always watched each other's backs, he and Joe. Tyce had talked Hattie into taking Joe in and teaching him the business, too.

They'd been having the time of their young lives, he and Joe, working together on covert tailing assignments, earning decent bucks, dating girls a little too high-class for their lowly backgrounds.

Tyce had thought himself in love. His girl had said she'd marry him. They'd made plans.

Her old man's thugs ambushed Joe and him with pipes, bottles and chains in an alley one night. The alley ran slick with blood. They'd barely survived the attack.

But they hadn't been the only ones hurt. He and Joe had grown up fighting in dark back alleys. They'd turned the weapons against their attackers. One of those men had died.

The cops blamed Joe. His fingerprints were found on the pipe that had crushed the skull of the meanest thug. They convicted him of murder. The old man used his political power to insure the toughest sentence possible. Till this day, Joe sat in a California prison, serving a life sentence without parole.

Pain and anger coursed through Tyce, making him sick and hot with it. He'd get Joe out, he swore. He'd spent the past fourteen years of his life trying. He'd built his fortune, a damn solid one, with just that end in mind. But money wasn't enough to get Joe's case reopened. The old man had too much power in California; he'd gone to great lengths to prevent discovery of his own role in the killing. He had, after all, hired those thugs. Joe had killed in self-defense.

During his quest for justice, Tyce had learned about other cases that cried out to him. Street punks, foster kids, teens thrown into jails without sufficient counsel or evidence. Tyce considered these kids his own. He knew the battles they fought, the odds they faced. He did what he could to help them. His investigations had gotten quite a few of them off.

It was Joe's turn now.

This assignment to follow Valentina Richmond promised to be the key to Joe's freedom. Tyce had struck a deal with her uncle, Edgar Richmond—another viable political force in California. Tyce would keep him informed of every move his niece made, and Edgar would see to it that Joe's case was retried.

Nothing could get in the way of that deal.

It took a while, but Tyce eventually slept. He opened his eyes hours later to bright Florida sunlight, the roar of the surf outside and a pang of annoyance. He'd slept much deeper than he'd intended.

He rose from the sofa bed, crossed the living room to the closed bedroom door and rapped on it, hoping Claire hadn't slipped by him unnoticed. Chances were she was still sleeping.

She'd been exhausted last night by the time they'd driven up to the beachside complex and hadn't put up more than a token fight when he'd registered them in a one-bedroom unit instead of a two bedroom. This setup would afford him a better watch over her. The sofa bed was situated near her bedroom door, allowing no way in—or out—without his notice.

Unless, of course, he was dead to the world.

His knock drew no response from within the bedroom. "Ms. Jones?" he called. He received no answer. Steeling himself against the odd rush of tenderness he'd felt when he'd used her given name last night, he called, "Claire?"

She didn't answer.

He tried the bedroom door, found it unlocked and pushed it open. The king-size bed was rumpled but unoccupied. The adjoining bathroom open and empty.

She was gone.

4

CURSING BENEATH HIS breath, Tyce strode from the bedroom to the kitchenette, then back to the sliding-glass doors in the living room. He whisked the drapes aside to find the chairs on the tenth-story balcony unoccupied, with no one standing at the railing that overlooked the sugar-white beach and azure Gulf waters.

Anger stormed through him, and he realized it was fueled by a keen anxiety. She'd left the condo without him. Anything could happen to her out there alone. Anything. Anyone as famous as she faced a very real danger on the streets unprotected.

Another thought hit him like a fist to the stomach—what if she wasn't coming back? Maybe his asinine slipup last night when he'd called her "Princess" had tipped her off to the fact that he knew her real identity. Maybe she'd caught a bus or a train, or rented a car.

She'd left a few toiletries and luggage, but she could have done so to throw him off, to get farther away before he realized she wasn't coming back. She had enough cash to buy whatever she needed and travel as far as she wanted to go.

Pacing to his briefcase, he took out his notebook computer, flipped it open and sat down at the glass dining table. With a few clicks of the mouse, he brought up a local street map on the screen, then activated the electronic tag he'd attached to her purse. He'd find her, by God.

A blinking red light on the screen indicated the location of the tag. She was still on the main beachside road, he realized with relief. He studied the map to pinpoint her exact location. When he found it, he frowned in puzzlement. The red light indicated the condo! The electronic device had to be *here*. Had she left her purse? Or had she discovered the tag and removed it? If so, he'd have a hell of a time tracking her down.

As he rose from his seat to search the condo for the purse or the tag, the front door opened. In walked Claire, her purse in one hand and plastic grocery bags in the other. The relief he felt at seeing her made him all the more angry.

"Morning!" she sang brightly. With her face shaded by those infernal sunglasses and her new sun hat, she looked like a typical young vacationer at the beach, buoyant and carefree and impossibly beautiful in slim white shorts and a flowered halter top.

"Where the hell have you been?" Tyce slammed his computer closed as she waltzed blithely by him on her way to the kitchenette.

"Oh, Walker, it was wonderful. I went to a grocery store." She took off her hat and sent it sailing to the sofa, freeing her curls to bounce and shimmer. "I tried to order breakfast from room service, but this place doesn't have room service, being a condominium complex instead of a hotel. The nearest restaurant is a few blocks away, but the concierge—I mean, the clerk—told me that a grocery store was just across the street. And we have a kitchen, Walker. It all just fell into place!"

"Don't you understand how dangerous it is for you to leave here without me?" His angry reprimand drew her attention away from the grocery bags she'd deposited onto the kitchen counter. She opened her mouth to reply, but he cut her off before she could say a word. "I'm supposed to be guarding you from the media and some crazy stalker. How the hell can I do that if you sneak out on your own?"

She pressed her lips together and lifted one elegant, golden brow above the rim of her sunglasses—a regal admonishment, he realized, for addressing her in an unseemly manner. "I believe I have the right to come and go as I please."

"Only if you *want* to be mobbed by reporters or shot by some rifle-toting nut!"

She paled, but her stance remained queenlike, with her head held high. "Neither of those fascinating possibilities rate very highly on my vacation roster. But then, I hadn't planned on having a constant shadow following me around everywhere, either."

It occurred to him then that this trip to Panama City might not have been as spontaneous as it had seemed. Maybe she'd meant to come here all along. Maybe she'd planned to meet someone.

Edgar Richmond had hired him to report on her activities; he may have had more reason than he'd mentioned. Had she just returned from an early morning rendezvous? The thought twisted and rankled inside of him. With whom, and why? A political intrigue? A secret lover?

He pried his gaze away from her, needing to cool down. Needing to lose the attitude. He had one, he knew—a bad one. He didn't like the idea of her sneaking away for a private tryst...with any damn body. And though it was his job to probe, question, monitor and report, he didn't want to doubt her truthfulness to him. He, who had personally uncovered hundreds of shady dealings and deceptions—especially among the famous, the wealthy and the beautiful—found himself ready to believe that she'd only gone to get groceries. What was happening to him?

"You scared the hell out of me," he muttered.

Some of the regal disdain left her voice. "I'm sorry." She pulled a carton of eggs out of a grocery bag, then a loaf of bread. "You were sleeping so soundly, I hated to wake you."

"I don't care if I'm in a coma. You wake me before you go anywhere."

She offered no reply, seemingly intent on putting a quart of milk in the refrigerator, but he noticed a renegade dimple playing hide-and-seek beside her mouth.

He narrowed his eyes. "What are you smiling at?"

She turned away to open a cupboard. "I'm not smiling."

"Okay, then what are you trying *not* to smile at?"

When she finally glanced back at him, her dimple had deepened. "You were actually *yelling* at me."

He frowned, unsure of how to reply. She didn't seem to be asking for an apology.

She leaned against the kitchen counter and propped her hand on a slender hip. "Do you know how long it's been since anyone has yelled at me? I believe the last person was my father, when I was about nine." She looked so pleased that the last of his anger evaporated. How could any woman enjoy being yelled at? Not that she had allowed it for very long. The look she'd given him at the time could have frozen any man's mouth shut. His ranting, he realized, hadn't affected her at all, other than to bring an amused dimple to her cheek.

Had it also brought a sparkle to her eyes, or maybe a defiant gleam? He wouldn't know. She was still hiding from him behind those sunglasses. Even last night, she'd escaped to her bedroom without removing them. He was almost ready to rip them off her face.

"I'm going to *cook*, Walker," she announced with a grand flourish of a spatula.

He settled back down into a chair at the table, crossed his arms over his chest and watched her. The woman was a true enigma. She threw herself into cooking breakfast with an anticipation usually reserved for adventures into the unknown.

"I'd hoped to make us poached eggs in Hollandaise sauce, Canadian bacon and toast with caviar and cream cheese, but I'm not sure how to make the sauce...or poach the eggs, for that matter. And do you know, I couldn't find Canadian bacon or a single jar of caviar in that entire grocery store?"

At first he thought she was kidding. When he realized she wasn't, he fought to suppress a smirk. Her princess side was showing. Who else would look for caviar in a beachside grocery store that probably specialized in beer, cheap wine, chips and sunscreen? Unable to resist teasing her, he exclaimed, "What, no caviar?"

"I know—it would have been perfect." Oblivious to his sarcasm, she made a disappointed moue and shrugged. "Oh, well. Guess we'll have to make do with bacon and eggs."

Make do turned out to be the operative phrase for that particular meal. Although he had offered helpful tips throughout the endeavor, the coffee was brewed to industrial strength, the bacon was charred and the eggs crunched with every few bites.

"I don't know how these shells could have gotten in here," she commented, frowning at the scrambled eggs on her plate. "I tried to be so careful."

"That's what you get for cooking with sunglasses on." His desire to see her eyes was turning into something of an obsession.

"They're prescription. I have to wear them." After another bite of burned bacon, she mumbled, "Sorry about the bacon."

"It's fine." Determinedly, he ate the rest of his.

"Liar."

He stopped chewing for a moment, tempted to retort, "If you're not the pot calling the kettle black!" But he didn't say it. She had as much reason as he to stick to the lies they'd told each other. She didn't need those sunglasses to see, she wasn't a prizewinning poet, and he hadn't been hired by her cousin. Yet, for all their lies, he had the damnedest feeling that he knew her—the important part of her. And he wanted very much to kiss her, right here and now, over their breakfast of burned bacon and crunchy eggs.

A dangerous impulse. She was a business assignment. An important one. Now was not the time to be sidetracked.

"Promise me," he uttered, "that you won't leave without me again."

Her fork paused above her plate, and she seemed to have a hard time swallowing. "I'm sorry, Walker," she finally replied in a soft, regretful tone. "I can't do that."

He stared at her. She stared back. He felt no anger at her refusal, only a deep uneasiness.

They finished what they could of their breakfast, then he helped her load the dishwasher. He'd be watching her constantly from this moment on. He wouldn't allow her to get away from him. Was she harboring some secret motive, he wondered, for leaving home alone and incognito? And why was he resisting the idea of making his first report on her whereabouts?

Because I want her to myself.

He pushed that disturbing thought away. He wasn't ready to make that first report because he didn't feel the time was right yet. "Will you answer me one thing, Claire?"

She paused in the act of drying her hands on a towel, looking almost frightened at his request. "What one thing?"

"If you know it's dangerous, why are you traveling alone?"

She bent her head to evade his searching gaze, finished drying her hands on the dish towel and hung it neatly, with great care, on a stove door rack. "I've recently broken up with my fiancé," she finally disclosed, her voice just above a whisper. "We went together for a long time. Our families were upset that I called off our wedding. I wanted to get away. To think." Slowly she lifted her face to his. "I came alone because I want my whereabouts to remain a secret. I didn't know who to trust."

He wanted, in that moment, to be the one she could trust.

But he wasn't.

A tentative smile curved her lips. "I think I made the right decision. I'm feeling better already, and I haven't even hit the beach." She turned on the dishwasher and cocked her head to one side, her hair tumbling over one silky shoulder as she studied him. "Are you going to just follow me around, or do you want to swim with me?"

Did he want to swim with her!

"I'm on duty." He knew he sounded too surly, too abrupt. "I'll just watch."

Her disappointment was almost tangible as she turned away, murmured something about changing and ducked into the bedroom.

He headed to the bathroom where he quickly shaved, changed into shorts and loaded a fresh cartridge into the microcamera built within the rim of his sunglasses. He'd promised Hattie pictures for her tabloid. He'd send her a few innocuous beach shots and be done with it.

And he'd report to his other client as soon as he found the chance.

Cued by the sound of her bedroom door opening, he returned to the living room the same time Claire did. She was wearing her sun hat, sunglasses and presumably the white bikini she'd bought yesterday, covered now by a white, loosely crocheted tunic that allowed teasing glimpses of the tanned skin beneath. The so-called cover-up barely reached the top of her smooth, golden thighs.

Shapely thighs. Shapely legs, somehow longer than he'd first thought. A man could get lost, wrapped in those endless legs....

He caught the beach towels she threw to him

and followed her to the elevator, his teeth once more tightly clenched. "Just watching" was going to be torture.

SAVORING THE SALTY TANG of the sea air and the bright, white heat of the Florida sun, Claire stood at the top of the stairway that led to the beach and enjoyed the panoramic beauty. Gulf water shimmered in shades of turquoise and blue, cresting in foamy waves against the white sand. Sea oats waved like wheat fields in the gulf breeze that whipped her hair around her face and cooled her sizzling skin in refreshing little spurts.

Nanny had told her about this beach in Panama City where she'd vacationed with her grandchildren. Out of all the spectacular beaches Claire had visited as Valentina Richmond—her favorites including Tahiti, St. Lucia and Kauai—she'd always longed to come to this one. Her uncle wouldn't hear of it, though. Her friends scoffed at the very idea. It simply wasn't one of their approved vacation sites. But Nanny had made the place sound so…friendly.

And it certainly seemed to be. The air hummed with the happy vibrations of sun-drenched vacationers: sand-covered children toddling from water to beach; scantily clad teens with slick, gleaming tans that smelled of coconut oil; women and men of all ages swimming, lounging and laughing, some sipping exotic rum drinks from the thatch-roofed bar beside the pool.

The best part, mused Claire, was that she stood

in the very center of the lively scene and no one knew or cared who she was. Wearing nothing but this skimpy white bikini and her sunglasses, she felt more comfortably concealed than she had in years. Not that she hadn't garnered a few admiring gazes from the men. Each lingering look flattered and soothed her sorely deflated feminine ego.

Thinking of that deflated ego, she turned a quick, covert gaze to Walker, who leaned with apparent languor against a shady column beneath the beach bar's thatched roof, presumably watching her from behind those silver sunglasses. Dressed in a pair of dark shorts that hugged his virile hips, he looked like some Roman sun god taking a leisurely break—his powerful body lean, tanned and well-honed. The impressive breadth of his shoulders and the rolling muscles of his biceps couldn't help but attract the feminine eye, which would then be drawn to the soft black curls that bisected his muscular chest and tapered down to a flat abdomen.

He was, in a word, gorgeous.

More than one woman around him had noticed. More than one preened and pranced, throwing come-hither glances in his direction. He'd smiled at a few, Claire had noticed.

He hadn't once smiled at her. The entire time she'd sunbathed on a lounge chair beside the pool, he hadn't paid much attention to her at all. "I'm on duty," he'd told her. She didn't see why that meant he couldn't sit with her. She'd given up the idea of swimming because she'd have to take off her glasses to do it. Instead she'd sufficed with quick, chest-high dips into the pool, just to cool herself down when she felt her skin beginning to bake.

But now she'd had enough of the pool, the sundeck and Walker's neglect. The beach and the wild blue sea beckoned.

Resisting another glance at Walker, she hurried down the smooth wooden steps from the sundeck to the beach, wondering if he'd follow. Of course he would. He was "on duty"—unless he'd become too distracted by one of the bathing beauties. Turning her face into the cooling sea breeze, Claire sank her feet into hot, powder-soft sand and trod toward the murmur of the surf.

She was here to have fun, to savor her freedom, to find out exactly what she'd been missing in her ivory tower. Why, then, should she waste another single, frustrating thought on Walker? She should be firing him now, anyway. The longer she stayed with him, the more chance she was taking that he'd hear about Valentina Richmond's running away and connect it to her cousin, who had hired him. She *had* to fire Walker...or maybe just slip away from him. That would be easier. She should leave him tonight.

Weaving between sand-digging tots and sunbathers, she made her way to the water's edge, where she burrowed her toes into the shifting wet sand, letting the waves surge, ebb and foam around her ankles. Kids on short, plastic Boogie boards rode the waves on their stomachs, gliding past her and clear up onto the sand. Mothers bobbed in the shallow water with their babies. Young couples clung together, laughing and jumping over waves.

A surprising ache of loneliness formed in Claire's throat. How could she feel so alone in the midst of such revelry? She gazed away from the young couples toward the cloudless azure sky, where gulls looped, helicopters lifted tourists above the coast for a panoramic view, and a small plane streamed a banner advertising evening specials at a local bar. Farther down the beach, a parasailer soared above the water with a colorful canvas chute billowing above him.

Life at its finest. Sun and fun and freedom.

"Watch out!"

The masculine yell startled her from very close behind. Strong hands caught at her arms and yanked her backward just as a young boy on a Boogie board shot across the water and onto the sand where she'd been standing. The kid would have mowed her down, she realized in a shaken daze, if she hadn't been dragged out of his path...and into her rescuer's strong arms, against a hard bare chest....

"Never say I didn't save you from anything." The deep, wryly amused mutter warmed her ear. Walker, of course. She'd recognized his touch before he'd spoken—and the masculine scent of his sun-heated skin, and her sensual response to both.

"From a sun-crazed ten-year-old on a Boogie board," she acknowledged, holding back a gurgle of laughter that sprang more from the pleasure of finding his arms around her than from true amusement. "You saved my life." She twisted around to look up at him, her cheek nearly touching his bare shoulder. "Or at least my ankles."

She caught his answering smile, and thrilled to it.

"Sorry, lady!" hollered the fair-haired youngster as he splashed by them with his board under one bony arm.

Walker slowly released her, backing away, leaving her feeling bereft. She wanted to touch him again, in any way she could. But he stood a full arm's length away, ankle-deep in the swirling surf, his eyes concealed behind silver sunglasses that reflected the turquoise water. "I thought you were going to swim."

"Changed my mind. I've decided to walk down the beach instead. Care to join me?"

"I won't be far behind you."

It wasn't the reply she'd wanted. Of course, she could hardly expect him to grab her hand, pull her against him and mosey along the shore with her as if they were lovers. He could have walked *with* her, though...as if he weren't being paid to. Maybe that was his point, she reflected as she paced a good distance ahead of him. To make it clear that he wasn't being paid to socialize with her.

She walked down the beach, the sun at her back

and sunbathers lounging on her right. Other walkers passed by, giving a nod and a smile. Some of the male walkers gave a bit more—long, appreciative gazes, soft whistles, an occasional "Mmm-mmm." She paid them no mind. The man whose attention she craved seemed oblivious to her, lurking somewhere far behind, probably watching bikini-clad bodies other than hers. She strode past huge hotel complexes, tropical gardens, swimming pools, beach bars and wooden-planked piers until she came to a cabana where a small crowd had gathered.

Jet Ski Rentals, the sign read.

She'd always wanted to try a Jet Ski.

"Walker!" She turned around and crossed the distance between them in a lively half skip. "Let's rent a Jet Ski."

HE'D KNOWN he should have refused the Jet Ski invitation, but by the time she'd turned to him with her exuberant request, his resistance to her had been ground down to a dangerous low.

He'd been watching her for hours as she sunned herself by the pool, nearly naked, with oil glinting all over her lithe body. She'd rubbed that oil onto her skin with slow, circular movements, stretching provocatively to reach out-of-the-way places. It had taken an excruciating effort to stop from offering his assistance. But he was no fool. A distraction like that would only take his mind off his job all the more. The job that had become more important to him than any other—protecting her. He'd managed to resist.

But then she'd risen from the lounge chair looking all flushed and disheveled, as if hot from a bout of lovemaking, and sauntered down to the sea, leaving her sun hat behind, allowing her hair to billow in a vibrant blaze around her golden shoulders. She moved with a seductive grace, tantalizing him and every man she passed. He felt insanely close to beating his chest and roaring out a savage warning to other male animals. *Keep your distance or die.*

He had a hell of a time keeping his own distance. His need to touch her had continued to grow until he'd pounced at the first excuse, grabbing her out of the way of a Boogie board when a simple shout would have done just as well. He'd savored the momentary contact. She'd felt warm, curvy and peach smooth, and he wanted to run his hands over her, everywhere.

He'd been in that frustrated state of self-deprivation when she'd asked him to take her Jet Skiing. Not even a warning of rough seas from the rental agent had stopped him.

That was how he came to be driving a roaring, vibrating monster over mountainous swells—up one side of a wave, then down to crash headlong into another, his muscles straining to hold the ski upright. The speed, the wind and the onslaught of water all added to the physical challenge of mastering the tumultuous sea.

Even more exhilarating was the feel of the

woman who clung to him—her arms around his waist, her thighs clamped around his and her torso pressed against his back. Her wet bikini seemed to have dissolved against his bare skin, and he felt every curvaceous contour as she leaned and shifted in sensuous synchrony with him. A wave jolted them from the side, and he swore he could feel the scrape of her sea-cooled nipples against his back.

Desire sluiced through him, and he took the next wave in a blind, heated rush. Water crested over their heads. He felt her shiver, and he yelled over the roar of the motor and the wind, "You okay?"

"Yeah!"

He couldn't help but smile. She was one plucky princess. And he was one crazy fool to have her out here. As they plunged down the side of another swell, he shouted, "Look to the right."

He sensed more than heard her exclamation. In the salty, sunlit spray around them shimmered a dazzling rainbow. The colors grew brighter, and awe overtook him. He was soaring through a misty prism with the woman he'd loved only in his dreams, riding headlong into a world of magic and passion and answered prayers.

Her arms tightened around him, and he ached to turn around and hold her. He couldn't, of course. And he couldn't keep her out here, riding rainbows. Angry at himself for a reason he didn't quite grasp, he turned the Jet Ski sharply toward the shore.

"Is our time up?" she shouted into the wind.

Although they'd rented the Jet Ski for a full hour and only half that time had elapsed, he answered, "Yep. Our time's up."

With every muscle tensed, he rammed the Jet Ski through the breaking surf until the front grazed the sand bottom. A lanky, sunburned teenager from the rental cabana ran out and grabbed hold of the ski as it bobbed and swayed. Tyce climbed down into the swirling, knee-high waves and reached up to help Claire. Her hair was a tangle of wet ringlets and her smile a flash of brilliance in her suntanned face as she laughingly fought to keep her balance on the bucking ski.

"Jump!" Tyce ordered, impatient to catch her. Impatient to fill his hands and arms with her....

She swung her long, slim leg over the seat, stood and fell into his outstretched arms. Her body slid down the length of his, her skin soft, slick and warm, sharpening his hunger, until her mouth was a mere whisper from his. His need to kiss her had grown into an urgent, living force, and as his eyes sought hers, a little shock went through him.

Gone were her sunglasses. He stared into wide, violet-blue eyes warm with laughter, sunshine and a powerful beauty that reached deep into his heart and squeezed. He felt suspended in time, in space...and more aroused than he'd ever been outside a bedroom.

He set her away from him, maybe a little too

forcefully. No woman had the right to affect him this much, especially one he could never, ever, have. Hurt bewilderment registered in her gaze, confusing him all the more. "Your glasses," he said. "They're gone."

Her lips parted, her hands flew to her face. "I've lost them! They must have fallen off."

"Wear mine." He whipped his glasses off and placed them on her, feeling both relieved and deprived as the lenses hid her eyes from him again. A momentary pang of anxiety attacked him as he remembered the pictures he'd taken of her with the microcamera in the sunglasses' frame. She wouldn't know the camera was there; it operated entirely by remote control from switches on his key ring. But the fact that the pictures were there—the sultry images he'd snapped of her throughout the day—rode heavy on his mind, just as frustration rode heavy in his gut. "I think we've had enough sun for today."

As he turned away from her and headed toward shore, intent on buying her another pair of glasses in the lobby gift shop then barricading her in her room—alone—she called from behind him, "Walker!"

Reluctantly he turned again to face her.

"Is there...anything you'd like to talk to me about? Or...ask me?"

After a blank moment, he realized the topic she was dancing around, the one that made her look so vulnerable and anxious. She wanted to know if he'd recognized her as Valentina Richmond.

"No. Should there be?"

She gazed at him for a long, uncertain moment. Children splashed in the waves a few feet away, sunbathers reclined behind them on shore, and an airplane flew its advertising banner in the azure sky below a late-afternoon sun.

Claire wished she could read his mind. *Had* he recognized her? Something certainly was bothering him. Something had made him put her aside just when she'd felt he would kiss her. She'd wanted that kiss. She hungered for it.

"It's getting late," he said. "We missed lunch. Let's grab a burger from the patio grill and take it up to the condo." Despite his plans that seemed to include her, he sounded cold. Bored. As if he wanted to be anywhere other than here, with her.

She knew then that he hadn't recognized her. Out of all the reactions people had when first meeting Valentina Richmond, the Perfume Princess, billionaire heiress, few were ever bored. If Walker had recognized her, his interest level would have gone considerably higher, she was sure, even if he'd try to mask it. The only thing he was trying to mask right now was his impatience to be gone from here. She wouldn't doubt that once they'd reach the condo, he'd retire to whatever room she wasn't in.

Anger tightened her fists. It wasn't fair that she should crave his touch, his kiss, when he wanted nothing at all from her. Especially after their closeness on the Jet Ski, closeness she'd felt had gone much further than even the physical. Although the shifting and flexing of muscle beneath sun-heated flesh had indeed contributed in a major way to her enjoyment—the mere memory made her knees weak—she'd felt as if she were part of him out there, as if their souls had been soaring together through that rainbow. Fanciful, she realized now. Was she *that* desperately lonely?

She lifted her chin, her pride rushing to her rescue. No. Infatuated, maybe, but not desperate. If she had to obsess about somebody, she'd find a man other than her bodyguard. A man who might actually return her interest.

"You go ahead and grab a hamburger," she suggested, trying not to sound resentful. "I'll meet you at the condo later." And before her attempt to stay reasonable wore thin, she sloshed through the waves toward the shore, angling sharply away from him.

"Claire."

She kept walking.

The sound of water swirling behind her warned of his approach. He caught her arm and swung her around. "Where are you going?"

"That's none of your business."

"Sorry, but it is."

"I can always rectify that." She met his green-eyed gaze. "I can fire you."

"Don't." His hands slid up her arms, his face darkening like a storm cloud, the scar across his cheek reminding her of lightning. "You need me, whether you admit it or not."

Oh, yes, she needed him. That was the problem. "There's only one thing I need," she said, her voice low but shaking, "and that's freedom to do as I please. It's what I came here for, Walker." And though she didn't mean to say it, the words tumbled out beneath his searching stare. "I have to figure out who I am...what I want out of life."

His frown deepened. "Like, going back to your fiancé?"

The question surprised her. She hadn't been sure he'd been paying attention when she'd told him earlier about breaking up with her fiancé. "No. That's one thing I'm sure of. But now I have to figure out what I *do* want to do."

"And you think you'll find the answer on this beach?" He sounded mildly scornful.

"I don't know where I'll find it, but I...I have to know what I've been missing!" She pulled back from his grasp, which seemed to have tightened. "I'm sorry if you're hungry or hot or bored. Do whatever makes you feel better. But I'm walking down this beach, and I'm finding a party. Yes, a party! And I'm going to dance, and drink, and make friends—"

"Friends!"

"And do whatever else I want to do. Is that clear?"

A muscle moved in his jaw. "Perfectly."

"Good." Straightening into a dignified stance, she turned and strode up onto the beach toward the pool deck. He followed her. And though she couldn't see him, she knew that an odd, powerful anger simmered within him. If ever a gaze could ignite a fire, she'd be in flames by now.

She stopped at the lounge chair where she'd dropped her beach bag, towel, hat and cover-up. Grabbing her short, crocheted tunic, she slipped into it and fastened a few buttons. Taking her compact out of her beach bag, she consulted the mirror as she combed the tangles from her half-dried hair, then slicked on a gleaming coat of lipstick. She would do exactly as she'd told him—find a lively beach party, make friends and have fun—or she'd die trying.

A shiver pierced her anger at that last thought. She'd rather *not* die trying.

But she'd seen no signs of stalkers or anyone following her since they'd lost the blue van back in Georgia. She'd escaped them all—the kooks and the paparazzi. She intended to enjoy every minute of the blessed respite.

Angling her makeup mirror for a covert look behind her, she saw that Walker stood at his earlier post near the bar, a formfitting black T-shirt now showcasing his muscled chest, his handsome face sullen, his sea-green gaze drilling holes through her.

Good. At least he was paying attention.

Leaving her hat and towel on the lounge chair, she sauntered across the deck, past the bar where Walker stood, and to the patio grill where an older man cooked hamburgers. "Two, please. With everything."

The chef smiled, fixed her hamburgers,

wrapped them in foil and handed them to her. She paid him and paced back to where Walker stood. Without a word, she thrust the burgers into his hands, then continued walking. From her side view, she saw him throw the burgers in a trash can and follow her.

Something told her he wasn't a happy camper.

She found the party she was looking for a short way down the beach. Music blared from the crowded deck of a beachside bar, couples shimmied and writhed on a dance floor, and a volleyball game kept a dozen men and a few young women laughing, running and jumping on the beach below.

Claire perched herself on a bar stool, crossed her legs and bought one of those exotic rum drinks with a pineapple slice on the side of a curvy glass. The first few sips went down smooth, cold and sweet. The rock 'n' roll made her body move. The teasing conversation between the bartender and his customers made her smile. And the fact that Walker loomed a short distance to her right made her feel ridiculously safe, safer than her usual army of bodyguards had ever made her feel, despite the fact that he looked ready to kill her.

She munched on pretzels, chatted with the portly, balding man beside her, and ordered another drink. Afternoon slipped into early evening; Tiki torches lit up the lounge and beach; the volleyball game played itself out. And all those strapping young men with their golden tans and athletic physiques swarmed around the bar, giving each other high fives and loudly roasting the losers. Claire soon found herself accompanied by two burly teammates who lost no time in pulling up stools beside her, introducing themselves, and making her feel thoroughly welcome.

Resisting an urge to crane her neck for another peek at Walker, she was surprised to find another of those wonderful rum drinks set in front of her...compliments of Kev and Dave. The party was promising to be a great one.

Conversation consisted of a few trite questions, silly jokes, and banter exchanged by the men. One of the Kev-Dave duo asked her to dance. On her way to the dance floor, she located Walker in the crowd and was pleased to see that he was still watching her. She chose a spot on the dance floor where she'd have an unimpeded view of him. And he of her. For safety reasons, she told herself. Why make his job harder than she had to? The fact that his silent gaze stirred her more profoundly than any of the other men's flattery had nothing to do with it....

After the second dance, she was feeling so relaxed in the hazy blue and green lights of the dance floor that she took off the sunglasses Walker had given her, sauntered to her place at the bar and slipped them into her bag. No one would recognize her here. She wasn't the same woman she'd been before. She was new, adventurous, mysterious...a nameless stranger in a good-time crowd.

Returning to the dance floor, she gave herself up to the fast, hard beat, alternating songs between Kev and Dave. As the music, the colored lights, the fragrant sea breeze and the exotic rum drink all worked together to loosen her muscles and her inhibitions, she found her gaze drifting again and again to the dark, silent man who stood at the side of the dance floor, his muscled arms crossed, his frowning eyes following the movement of her body. And when their gazes connected, an electric thrill coursed down her spine, warming every part of her.

Though she danced with partners who lavished her with all the attention a woman could want, she watched Walker. And he watched her. And her body moved for him—her hips, her shoulders, her heart. She wanted him, she realized. Only him. No one else would do.

When Kev broke in to replace Dave as her partner, she barely noticed.

Tyce noticed. He noticed every move made by her and the men surrounding her. Whether she knew it or not—and he didn't think she did—she'd claimed the undivided attention of quite a few. Though her dancing was little more than subtle gyrations in time to the music, she was too damn sexy to move that way without inciting some form of riot. And even though swimwear seemed to be the apparel of choice for this beach crowd, she drew more than her share of attention in her bikini and loosely crocheted tunic. If the

Florida summer night was usually hot, she'd raised the temperature by a few dozen degrees.

He wanted her so badly he could barely breathe.

And so did the other horny bastards who followed the sway of her hips, straining their eyes to see through the coarse netting of her tunic, drooling at flashes of lean, suntanned skin…and the long expanse of leg below. Tyce stood tensed, poised and hair-trigger ready for the first slobbering fool who made a move to touch her.

The pressure building within him increased as she shared a smile with her dance partner. The creep was nearly bursting at the seams to get his hands on her. To get lucky. A sudden doubt stuck in Tyce's craw. *Would* he get lucky? A vision blinded him for a gut-twisting moment: Claire taking some guy back to the condo with her… closing her bedroom door….

I have to know what I've been missing, she'd said.

His mouth went dry. The music had changed to a slow song and the lights had mellowed to a sultry violet that reminded him of her eyes. She wasn't returning to her seat at the bar. She was going to dance this love song in some man's arms. Some man who would hold her close.

Dancers on the floor paired off into couples. Without conscious thought, Tyce moved through the crowd, hungry and silent as a shark. She stood surprisingly still as the dance began, her eyes wide and her face flushed. As he drew closer, he realized why. Two young toughs beside her both seemed to have the same cozy idea in mind.

"This is my dance," one of them claimed.

"Beat it, Kev. I was here first."

"You had your turn, Dave. It's mine now."

"Please don't argue," Claire interjected, her cheeks flaming at the glances they were drawing from other dancers. "I think I'd rather sit this one out."

"She promised me this dance," Kev growled at Dave.

Worry clutched at Claire. Surely these two wouldn't fight over a simple dance. Would they? Dave's debonair smile was somewhat ruined by the clenching of his teeth, and Claire realized with a sinking heart that they just might fight.

"It's my turn," insisted Dave, reaching for her.

"'Fraid not." The challenge came from behind the two men, and both turned around to confront the interloper. Claire felt her heart expand with relief—and something more—as Walker shouldered his way between them, his dark, rugged face blazing with an inner intensity. He hooked a confident hand around her waist and pulled her into his arms. "This one's mine."

His gaze pressed that claim further, thoroughly possessing her.

Dave yelled, "Hey!"

Kev started. "Who the hell—"

"And if you two don't sit down," Walker warned in that quiet, iron-smooth drawl that raised the hairs on her arms as he shifted his gaze to the protestors, "you'll be mine, too."

Maybe it was the curbed violence that smoldered behind his eyes, or the deadly threat coiled within his tensed muscles, but to Claire's amazement, the two rivals stepped back, muttered curses beneath their breath and skulked off the dance floor.

With the same simmering intensity that had sent them on their way, Walker turned his attention to her. The night, for Claire, had suddenly taken on a deeper shade of magic.

"What are you doing here, lady," he asked hoarsely, fitting her against him, "driving all these gentlemen wild?"

"Dancing," she breathed, her voice lost to the sensual feel of his muscle-hardened body pressing hers into slow, rhythmic movement. A dance, only a dance, but the pleasure coursing through her somehow made it more. She was his for now; caught in his heated, virile embrace—and the mesmerizing power of his stare.

"Looked like you were doing more than that."

She tilted her head back and arched a brow, feeling much more womanly and desirable than she had all night. Or maybe all year. Or maybe all her life. "Did it look like I was being…naughty?"

"I'd say you were headed that way."

Her lips curled in enjoyment. His gaze lowered to her mouth and lingered there—intently so— until a serious heat washed through her. "I told you from the start," she whispered, "I want to be bad."

"Bad." He angled his face intimately toward hers. "With a man?"

"Yes. With a man."

He led her in a turn, his hand hard, warm and controlling at the small of her back. "In case you've been too busy to notice—" his gaze intensified "—I'm a man."

The hunger in his eyes took her breath away. Inexplicably, fear touched her, even as her pulse quickened with answering desire. He was dangerous; much more so than she'd realized before. "But you're *hired* to be with me," she said, searching for the reason she'd come to this bar, the reason she'd danced with men she'd barely seen. "I want someone who…*wants* to be with me."

His whisper was a heated growl against her mouth. "I want to be."

Desire suffused her, making her dizzy, muting her voice, leaving only her eyes to speak for her. His arms tightened around her and, without another word, he guided her off the dance floor.

5

HE WHISKED HER through the star-studded night, her sandals barely touching the darkened beach. Music and light spilled like waves from the hotel bars they passed, and the sea whispered secrets in the summer darkness.

Walker wanted her. The pressure of his arm around her, the urgency of his gait, the heat radiating from him in palpable waves, all thrilled her in a deep, elemental way...and at the same time, frightened her.

She knew nothing about pleasing a man. She wasn't sure she had ever pleased her fiancé. What made her think she could satisfy a man as street-wise and virile as Walker? Her appeal was only an illusion, a larger-than-life image with more flash than substance.

She slowed as they reached the lobby of their condo, her fear engulfing her. "Walker..."

But an elevator had opened, and without stopping for as much as a questioning glance, he swept her onto it. "Walker," she tried again, her stomach clenching, her throat tight and dry. "When I said I wanted to be *bad*...well, my meaning of the word might not exactly match yours."

The doors slid closed, like a well-oiled trap.

He turned to her, and his green-fire stare backed her up against the elevator wall. "Thanks for the warning, Claire." Leaning close, he braced a dark, muscled arm on either side of her. "I'll try not to let you shock me."

The humor in his gaze was quickly overpowered by smoky, turbulent desire. That desire overpowered her, too, making her feel faint with longing. Oh, but she did want him! She wanted to submerge herself in his fire, his strength, until she found—what? *What?* She didn't know, but she yearned for it. Her gaze shifted and danced with his, a mutual searching, until she felt her very soul drawn from her depths.

He took her mouth in a kiss that stunned her.

There was no gentleness in it. No courting, no teasing. Only heat and need and a raw sexuality that cut to the core of the issue. Her own need flared in immediate response, shocking her with its carnal intensity. She'd never been kissed like this before, if that's what it was, this deep, hot mating of mouths. She'd never feasted this way before, her hunger roused by the taste of him.

She wanted more, and angled her head to get it. He clutched her fiercely against him and drove his tongue in erotic rhythm. A rush of sensation washed away all thought.

With some distant part of her mind, she realized the elevator had stopped and the doors had opened. Vaguely she heard voices. Without breaking his mouth from hers, Walker hit at a button. The doors closed, shutting out the intruders. The elevator continued its climb.

Their kiss slowed into long, savoring tastes. His hands slid beneath her tunic, warm and roaming, caressing her everywhere except the places covered by her scant bikini. Those places began to throb for his attention.

He soon gave it, at least to her breasts, where his fingers splayed, rubbed and piqued her to hardness through the thin fabric of her bikini top. Pleasure flashed in quicksilver pangs that made her tremble. He filled his palms with her breasts, wedging the hardened crests between his fingers, and continued to kiss her.

The elevator stopped again.

"We've got to get to the condo," he rasped.

She nodded in dazed agreement.

His hands swept downward and curved around her bottom, lifting her. Her legs folded around his hips. His male hardness lodged solidly between their bodies, growing all the larger, straining against the fabric of his shorts. She couldn't help but move against it. Sweat beaded on his face; a groan tore from his throat, and with urgent strides, he bore her down the hall.

She thrust her fingers into his silky black hair and kissed him.

Distracted by the kiss, he braced her against their condo door and undulated against her. With a surprised gasp, she countered the move. He gritted his teeth and cursed. Their gazes met in heated communion. They had to get inside...lose the clothes....

He removed one hand from where he held her—where his hard, blunt fingertips had pressed beneath the edges of her bikini bottom—and shoved the key into the lock. She didn't help matters. As he carried her inside, she engaged him in another voluptuous kiss. A tortured moan erupted from him, and he struggled to lock the door. She half expected him to stop at the sofa, or even lower her to the floor, but he persevered all the way to the bedroom.

He tumbled her onto the bed, stood beside it and yanked off his shirt. Her fingers flew to the buttons of her netted tunic. Flinging his shirt aside, he caught her wrists and pressed them back against the pillows. "Don't take anything off," he commanded. "Let me." After a short, searing stare, he added hoarsely, "I've been wanting to do it all day."

He turned on the bedside lamp and stripped off the rest of his clothes.

With her heart pounding, Claire lay obediently still against the pillows, arrested by the dark, male beauty of his body as he revealed it. She remembered well his sinewy arms and torso from their day on the beach, but when he unzipped his shorts and pushed them down his powerful thighs, her breath caught almost painfully. He was huge, vibrant and glistening in the golden lamplight, his body hardened for lovemaking.

He knelt on the bed, straddled her thighs, and

reached for the buttons of her tunic. He tugged them loose, one after the other, his rugged face taut with need. Laying open the tunic, he levered his body just above hers, his forearms trapping her hands in the netting.

A disturbing glint shone in his heated stare. "You know the hell you put me through, don't you, trying to get us inside this condo?"

"Hell?" she whispered, not quite understanding.

"Payback, or so I've heard—" he nudged his slightly abrasive chin down the sensitive curve of her neck "—is also hell."

While he held her hands entangled in her tunic, he seared a tingling path to her shoulders and then to her breasts with kisses, half bites and ingenious tongue strokes that drove her slowly, steadily, into a throbbing heat. He was playing with her, it seemed...yet, *not* playing—edging around the small triangles of her bikini top with his tongue, flicking occasionally across their middles, making her want in a way she'd never dreamed of wanting...in a feverish, desperate way. When his lips tugged her nipples into long, hard buds through the thin cotton, she cried out at the piercing pleasure and arched high off the bed, struggling to push the fabric aside and feel his mouth on her.

His eyes were dazed by the time he lifted his head and reached around her to unhook her top. He pulled it off of her with urgent tugs, and when he'd freed her from it, he branded her with a smoldering gaze. "Claire..." he breathed. "You're beautiful." He lowered his head to her again, expelling hot, unsteady breaths, and reverently laved first one breast, then the other.

He forgot all about trapping her arms as he moved down to her bikini panties. He applied the same teasing tactics, though, using not only his mouth, but his fingers and thumbs, until she writhed in wild undulations, gasping and quaking with the need for his body.

He stripped the swimsuit down her legs, then rose onto his knees between them. Gripping her hips, he pushed solidly, deeply, into her.

The sensation momentarily stunned her. He'd stretched her with an incredible hardness; filled her to an impossible fullness. She thought she'd explode from the pleasure. As he began to move in slow gyrations, the pleasure leaped and glowed, then coursed in heated torrents throughout her body. Her mouth opened. Tears formed in her eyes. She lifted her hips to meet his thrusts.

It could have been anger or hostility that twisted his features, made a muscle clench in his jaw, but it was need—passionate need—*for her*. The knowledge infused her with an uncanny power. She used that power to stoke his need.

A fine sheen glistened on his face and on every straining muscle of his magnificent body as she matched and countered his thrusts. His gaze sought hers, and he reached for her—pulled her up from the mattress, caught her to him in a hard embrace. The move forced a deeper penetration. Pleasure nearly blinded her.

His gaze probed deep. Soul deep. "Dance with me now, Princess." His gruff whisper inflamed her. Her fingers dug into hard muscle at his shoulders as she worked her hips. And he worked his. A ragged cry escaped her.

Tyce captured her mouth in a frenzied kiss. Their rhythm quickened with such synchronized precision he thought he might go mad. She was more than he'd bargained for. More than he'd known existed. He'd wanted sex from her, nothing more. Not this need. Not this urgency. Not this certainty gunning through him as he kissed her, as he loved her, that she was his—*only* his—and he would die if she wasn't.

She clutched him fiercely, and with a wild cry, spasmed around him in a shuddering climax. He lost himself then in the stabbing, white-hot thrall of a pleasure too keen to contain. And when they at last tumbled together to the mattress—gasping, panting, and quaking in each other's arms—he was too stunned to speak.

A few hundred heartbeats later, when the worst of the shock had worn off, she stirred in his arms, soft and slender against him, and her whisper rasped against his ear. "Was it as bad for you as it was for me?"

He didn't smile. He couldn't if he tried.

"Yeah," he muttered, tightening his arms around her. "It was bad."

HE AWOKE in the morning alone on the living room sofa bed. He'd left the warmth and temptation of Claire's dewy, naked body shortly after she'd drifted off to sleep last night. It hadn't been easy, extricating himself from her long, velvet-smooth legs that had interwoven with his. Hadn't been easy, denying himself the pleasure of sleeping with her in his arms.

But he couldn't, in all good conscience, remain another minute in her bed. He hadn't had any business being there to start with. There were too many lies between them. Big lies.

She believed him to be her bodyguard, and to have been hired by her cousin. Even though she wouldn't be talking to John Peterson anytime soon for fear of having the call traced, she would eventually discover the deception. John *had* hired a man from a security company to meet her at the airport and drive her around. Tyce had sent one of his own female operatives in a curly auburn wig and sunglasses to meet the driver at the airport. He'd driven the imposter heiress to a posh hotel, where she'd promptly dismissed him. Tyce could just imagine a possible conversation between Claire and her cousin. "Dismissed my bodyguard? I did no such thing! He's with me now..."

But she wouldn't call her cousin for a few more weeks, according to their taped conversation. And Tyce wouldn't be staying with her that long. Once he'd determined her purpose in fleeing and her planned destination, he'd be finalizing his reports and turning her protection back into her uncle's capable hands.

The idea of turning her over to anyone bothered him a little too much. Almost as much as his conscience bothered him. He'd deceived her... and hadn't let that deception stop him from taking her to bed. Of course, she hadn't let *her* lies stop her, either. She'd made love to him under an assumed identity.

That thought also disturbed him too much. Grabbing fresh clothes from his suitcase, he strode to the bathroom for a shower. Regardless of the lies she'd told him, nothing could excuse his lapse in self-control. He had to get their relationship back on its proper footing.

He'd already compromised his case. He'd become sexually involved with the subject of his investigation. A man's freedom hinged on his successful completion of this case—Joe's freedom. He'd jeopardized that all-important, longtime goal for one night in her bed.

One night in her bed. There would never be another.

Stepping under the shower spray, he tried to forget the intoxicating taste of her mouth, her body. The feel of her in his arms. The incredible rightness of being inside her. With a muttered curse, he turned the shower to cold and directed his thoughts to his immediate obligations.

One loomed ahead of him with disturbing new dimensions: he was obligated to report her whereabouts and her activities, including those of an intimate nature, to her uncle. Edgar Richmond seemed to believe that some malevolent outside influence had spurred her outrageous behavior. He wanted to know why she'd run away, and if she was involved with someone.

She was definitely involved with someone now.

Shoot me, someone, Tyce silently moaned, *and put me out of my misery.* He finished showering, shaving and dressing in a state of mortification. The situation called for some form of damage control, but he couldn't decide on the right approach. If he resorted to following his natural inclination, he'd come clean. Tell her everything. Apologize.

But he'd be betraying his client and failing Joe. And for what? Claire would only rush out into the world alone, upset and unprotected, and therefore, more vulnerable than ever. Just remembering her on the dance floor surrounded by hungry, salivating wolves made him reluctant to cut her adrift. *I want to know what I've been missing,* she'd told him.

Had she found it?

What if she hadn't?

What if she had?

Growing more confused with every question, he left the bathroom through the doorway that led to the living room, *not* the one that led to the bedroom. She could still be sleeping in there, tangled in the sheets—naked, willing, and compellingly beautiful. He couldn't allow himself to go anywhere near the bedroom. As he concentrated on maintaining that resolve, he walked directly into the woman he swore to avoid.

"Oh!" she exclaimed, dropping her leather toiletry case to the living room floor and reeling from the impact of their collision. "Excuse me!"

Tyce caught her shoulders to steady her. Her hair, tangled and matted from last night's wild interlude, felt silky beneath his hands and glimmered golden with strawberry highlights in the morning sun. The blue velour robe sashed about her slender form accentuated the blueness of her eyes—bewitching eyes, now shaded with unmistakable self-consciousness. Apparently she wasn't used to morning afters.

"I must look a mess," she said with an awkward little laugh, her hand delving into her hair. "I haven't even—"

"You look fine." *Too fine.* She looked soft, feminine and irresistibly touchable in her morning dishevelment, her face flushed with shyness. Forcing his hands away from her, he fought the urge to pull her into his arms and kiss away that shyness.

"The other door to the bathroom was locked," she explained in a breathless rush, "so I—"

"Sorry, I forgot to unlock it."

"Then I saw the sofa bed pulled out," she continued, "and I was so surprised to realize you slept there that I didn't pay attention to where I—"

"*I* ran into *you.* I should have been the one watching—"

"But I guess I can understand why you slept out here. I mean, I'm probably not the easiest person to sleep with."

That brought them both to a pause.

Feeling her face blaze with embarrassment, Claire ducked her head and bent to retrieve her toiletry case. *He'd left her bed to sleep in the living room.* She still felt stunned and inexplicably hurt at that discovery.

Walker swept up the toiletry case before she reached it and handed it to her. Their hands touched, their gazes met. His eyes were unreadable now. Gone were all traces of the passion that had burned there last night. But his urgent plea still echoed in her heart. *Dance with me now, Princess.* Never had the sound of that word thrilled her more. She'd known he'd meant it as an endearment—an oddly personalized endearment that had nothing to do with her public persona. And in the heat of their lovemaking, she'd felt an awesome connection with him, an almost spiritual sense of oneness. Could that connection have been a sex-induced delusion on her part?

"I slept out here," he gently informed her, "to guard you. I have a job to do."

"It's okay, you don't have to explain." Claire forced a smile and backed away toward the sanctuary of the bathroom. Why couldn't she just shut up and run? He'd obviously had his fill of her last night. "I probably hogged the whole bed. It's been so long since I've slept with anyone." *Dumb thing to say! He didn't need to know that!*

"Claire—" He took a step toward her.

She escaped into the bathroom before he could touch her again, or spout another excuse for having left her bed. Closing the bathroom door, she leaned against it, her heart thudding. She'd made a complete fool of herself.

If only the sight of that rumpled sofa bed hadn't jarred her so. But she'd woken with a powerful craving to feel his arms around her again. She'd been surprised and disappointed to find him absent. She'd thought he might have gone to make coffee, or to freshen himself in the bathroom. It never occurred to her that he hadn't planned on returning to bed. She'd felt so sure that he'd come back to her. To claim at least one more dance.

She'd been wrong.

And here she was, propped against the bathroom door, mortified by her own overreaction to their lovemaking. She'd never dreamed it could rattle her this much. It hadn't been the physical things they'd done, she realized, that had shaken her so profoundly. It had been the passion flowing stronger and wilder with every kiss, every move. Afterward, an equally charged feeling had radiated between them, binding her to him in a glowing tenderness.

Or so she'd thought. But if he'd felt it, too, why would he have slept elsewhere? Why would he have reverted back to the trusty, protective shadow, perpetually "on duty"?

Because that's who he was—a shadow paid to protect her.

Pulling away from the door, she set her toiletry case on the marble-topped vanity and strove for emotional control. Why should she care where Walker slept? She'd wanted to know what she'd been missing, and he'd showed her. Wild, uninhibited sex—that's what she'd been missing. She should thank him for the insight and move on.

Move on.

Gazing at herself in the mirror with forlorn dismay, she realized that the time had come. The story of her running away had probably hit the tabloids by now, and maybe even the mainstream press. He'd surely recognize her then. One blissful night in his arms didn't mean she could trust him to keep her whereabouts a secret. Did it?

She wanted it to mean precisely that. She wanted to tell him her real identity and explain her need to be free, to find herself, to determine her course for the future. The answers she was seeking seemed no closer. In fact, she was more confused than before. One thing she couldn't lose sight of was that no one could be trusted. That had to include Walker.

Surprised by the fresh pain that long-held knowledge evoked, she decided she'd better pack immediately after she'd showered and dressed. She should be thanking him for leaving her bed.

Heaven knew *she* couldn't have been the one to leave it.

WHILE HE WAITED for her to rejoin him, Tyce took the opportunity to send his first report to Edgar Richmond. He hooked up the modem of his notebook computer to the living room phone jack, typed in a coded message and sent it via E-mail. The report told her general location and assured that she was safe. He also reported that, as of yet, she'd met with no one.

He did not mention last night's activities. As far as Tyce was concerned, their night together had been no one else's business. He also realized that he wouldn't have reported her private activities even if she'd chosen another man. Her uncle may have had a valid need to know if she was involved with a potentially dangerous crowd, or if her private affairs could in some way harm his or her future. But Tyce saw no evidence of intrigue...and he'd never been one to kiss and tell.

When he'd finished his report and packed his computer back into his briefcase, he stepped out onto the veranda and called Fred on his cell phone. Quietly he dictated the coordinates of their location on the map in a code that only he would understand. Tyce wanted backup close at hand. Fred and a small crew of handpicked security agents would establish a mobile perimeter in the immediate vicinity to keep a lookout for anything or anyone suspicious. In a place as wildly populated with teens, tourists and college students as Panama City in the summertime, their job would be close to impossible, since "suspicious behavior" was the norm. Tyce wanted a crew in place, just the same. He wanted to take no chances with her safety.

He'd slipped his cell phone back into his pocket and returned to the living room only moments before she emerged from the bedroom. Dressed this time in a mint-green halter top and jean shorts, her hair a shiny halo of curls, she sported another pair of large, round sunglasses.

He rose slowly up from the sofa, struck anew by her vibrant beauty. He was also struck by his own dismay at having her eyes hidden from him again. "Where'd you get the glasses?"

"I had an extra pair that I bought at Value Village, in my suitcase. I looked in my beach bag for the pair you lent me yesterday, but—" She bit her lip and grimaced, looking remorseful and charming. "It seems I've lost them. They weren't in there. I'll pay you for them." She dipped into her purse and came out with a handful of bills.

"Forget it. I've got another pair in the car." *But not with a microcamera hidden in the frame.* Whoever might find them wouldn't know the camera was there; wouldn't find the pictures he'd taken of her...he hoped.

"No, really, I want to reimburse you."

When she stepped toward him with the money, he saw her luggage in the doorway behind her, packed and stacked on its built-in luggage cart.

Something moved uncomfortably in his chest. He asked, "Are we going somewhere?"

She halted a short distance away from him, andthe question hung in the air. "I'm sorry, Walker," she finally replied, her tone soft with regret. "You've been...wonderful." The last word sounded a little choked, and she looked away from him. "You helped me escape from the bad guys, and took great care of me. Now it's time for me to move on." She ended on a bleak whisper, "Alone."

The discomfort in his chest turned into a definite pull. She meant to leave him. She handed him the money for the lost sunglasses. He ignored her outstretched hand. "It's too dangerous for you to travel alone."

"I'll be careful."

"Not good enough." He saw her mouth tighten and her chin raise, but he pressed on anyway. "Where will you go? What will you do?"

"I'd rather not say."

"Will you take a bus, or train, or...what?"

"Train, probably. But right now I'm going to call a taxi." She shoved the handful of money against his chest. "Here, please take this."

"I don't want the money, Claire." He wanted answers. Wanted to know where she was going, what she was doing. Wanted to hear the truth about her identity. "How long do you plan to keep running?"

Her lips parted in alarm. He was pushing her further than she'd wanted to go with this conversation. The reply seemed to be dragged unwillingly out of her. "Until I find myself."

"Care to explain that?" He searched her face, willing her to confide in him. He didn't stop to consider why he wanted her to, or what he'd do with the information.

She closed her eyes. "There are things about me you don't understand."

"So fill me in."

"I can't!" Her anguished gaze clashed with his. "I'm sorry. I'm just...not the person you think I am."

"Do you mean that in a figurative sense or...that you're not Claire Jones?"

A little sound of distress escaped her and she reached for the phone. "I've got to call a taxi."

He caught her wrist above the telephone. "You need me, Claire, no matter who you are."

They stared at each other for an awkward moment. "I don't want to need you."

And he didn't want to need her. But he couldn't let her leave like this. "Go with me to a gift shop," he said, playing for time. "You can buy me a pair of sunglasses. Then I'll take you to a train station."

"You want me to buy you a pair of sunglasses *now*?"

"Yes, now."

She swallowed, her throat visibly working. "Okay. We'll go to a gift shop and buy your glasses...but then we'll say goodbye."

Conscious of her racing pulse beneath his fingers, he slowly released her wrist. "It'll take me only a minute to get my things." Hoarsely he added, "Don't you dare leave without me." He returned in minutes with his overnight bag and briefcase. She stood near the sliding-glass doors, gazing out over the Gulf. "Do you have everything?" he asked her.

She nodded, and he rolled their luggage out the door. As they stepped into the hallway, a young man in a Hawaiian shirt and shorts brushed rudely past them. Tyce frowned and watched him disappear around a corner. Something about the guy's movement struck him as odd. It was almost as if he'd been waiting outside their door....

"Walker, look!" Claire called in surprise, pointing to a silver object on the hallway floor.

His sunglasses. He bent and scooped them up.

"I guess they must have fallen out of my bag," she said.

As their gazes met, a deep blush climbed into her cheeks. A dull, throbbing warmth seeped into his blood. "Last night," he whispered.

They both knew when. The memory flared to life between them, binding them in its heat: him pushing her up against the door with an urgent kiss, almost making love to her right there in the corridor. And he wanted to do it again.

"You've got your sunglasses back now," she whispered unevenly, backing a step away from him. "No need to go to a gift shop. I...guess I'll call a taxi from the lobby."

"Have breakfast with me."

Claire felt her heart turn over beneath his compelling stare. She couldn't think straight, standing this close to him in the place where they'd incited each other to a frenzy. "I don't think I—"

He laid a finger across her lips to stop the refusal from forming. Warm reaction sizzled through her. Gruffly he demanded, "Don't you think what we had last night warrants at least a breakfast?"

It was unfair of him, and they both knew it. But the question was out there now. She couldn't ignore it. And she didn't want to lie. Not about this.

What they'd had last night warranted much more than a breakfast.

6

THEY DROVE WEST, far beyond the city limits, leaving behind the crowded beaches, amusement parks and tourist shops. When at last the commercial strip gave way to moss-draped coastal forest, Walker stopped at an isolated but cheery roadside diner.

They hadn't spoken much in the car. Claire's heart had grown heavy at the thought of saying goodbye to him again. He'd made it impossible at the condo. She'd have to be stronger than that when the time came to leave him after breakfast. She'd have to ignore anything he might say and stick to her plan of calling a taxi.

At least she would have this last meal with him. It warmed her to think that he'd insisted on it. Truth be told, it warmed her just to be with him. How could she have allowed herself to become so...*intense* with someone she'd planned to leave from the very start?

With his hands light and guiding at her waist, he ushered her past groups of chatting customers to a white-topped table for two. Beside them at a dining counter, construction workers sat on stools sipping coffee, eating breakfast and idly watching a small television perched above them in a corner.

Claire hoped she would be far away by the time Walker learned of her deception. She didn't want to see how he'd take the news about her real identity...whether he'd be hurt that she'd lied, or amused at her ruse, or gratified that he'd have a juicy story to tell his friends. And if he ever profited from that juicy story, she didn't want to know about it.

A plump waitress with tired-looking eyes took their order, yelled it out to the cook and poured them coffee.

"So tell me," Walker said after the waitress had moved on to another table, "where can I get a volume of your poetry, and which one would you recommend I start with?"

She gazed blankly at him. Poetry? She then remembered the role of prizewinning poet she'd assumed at the airport. Somehow it wasn't quite as easy lying to Walker about it now as it had been then. "I wouldn't recommend any of my poetry."

He lifted a brow, and she sensed a seriousness in him that far outweighed the whimsical subject of poetry. "Why not?"

She glanced away, feeling guilty for all the lies. If only she'd met him under different circumstances. If only she really were Claire Jones. She tried to inject a breeziness into her tone. "You hated the one I recited for you, remember?"

No reminiscent smile lightened his gaze. "You

are poetry, Claire. Don't let anyone make you forget that while you're...running around looking for yourself."

Her throat tightened, and she felt like crying. Even though she'd sworn she didn't need his approval, she'd wanted to win it. Now he seemed to be giving it to her, all ten million megawatts of it. But she recognized the compliment for what it was: his way of saying goodbye.

The waitress delivered steaming plates of omelettes, grits and toast. Though she wasn't hungry, Claire forced herself to eat. She needed a distraction from the emotions warring inside her. As she spread jelly on her toast, the television caught her attention—a morning newscast.

"For all you celebrity watchers, more news from the Richmond mansion..." announced a perky brunette anchorwoman with a humorous lilt. "The Perfume Princess gave her bodyguards the slip. We take you now to the Los Angeles department store where Valentina Richmond mysteriously vanished last Thursday."

Claire dropped her knife to the table with a clatter, cringed at the glances thrown her way, and swung a panicked gaze to Walker. She had to get out of there, *now.* "Walker, I'm not feeling well. I want to leave."

She started to rise, but he caught her hand and forced her to stay seated. His attention had been snagged by pictures on the television screen. With a sinking heart, Claire turned reluctant eyes to a video of herself, obviously taken by the de-

partment store security cameras as she walked
past her unsuspecting bodyguards and headed
for freedom. With her hair in strawberry-blond
curls—as it was now—she wore her yellow
T-shirt, denim shorts and tortoiseshell sunglasses. She had, of course, arrived at the airport
looking exactly that way when Walker had met
her.

"Could this mystery gal really be our Perfume
Princess?" quipped the on-scene reporter. A
photo flashed beside it of Claire in a formal ball-
gown with diamonds in her pale-blond upsweep.

Walker's hand, she noticed, had tightened on
hers, but he hadn't torn his gaze from the screen.

"Rumors have been confirmed that heiress Valentina Richmond vanished from this upscale department store Thursday, slipping away from her
bodyguards as they waited for her outside a rest
room. They found only her beige satin slip, which
she'd left hanging on a hook."

Choking back a hysterical giggle, Claire an-
chored the elbow of her free arm on the table and
pressed a trembling fist to her mouth. She hadn't
realized she'd left her slip.

Across the photos flashed the headline Valentina Gives Guards The Slip. Who, she wondered,
came up with headlines like that? Did they grad-
uate from headline-writing school with an A in
punmanship?

With her face hot and her pulse a dull roar in
her ears, she prayed that the newscast would finish quickly with her, but the story dragged on. Although they acknowledged the existence of the

note she'd left for her uncle, which had merely stated her need to get away by herself, they ruminated on the possibility of a kidnapping. The photos then switched to various locales, showing the Beverly Hills mansion her mother had designed, the New York town house where her grandfather had lived, the villa in the south of France where she'd entertained her so-called friends, the yacht her father had loved, and quick flashes of the other vacation cottages around the globe that she'd inherited. Although she knew she owned them all, she felt as if they belonged to someone else.

"She hasn't been seen," the anchorwoman finished, "at any of her usual hangouts. If you have a tip about Valentina's disappearance, call our news hotline."

Claire bent her head and concentrated on keeping her face averted from as many people as possible. She couldn't, however, hide from Walker. She braced herself for the inevitable glint of surprise she'd see on his face...possibly even shock...and whatever other emotions had been stirred by the discovery that he'd been intimate with the world-famous Valentina Richmond.

An ache formed near her heart. She didn't think she could take it, if his interest suddenly intensified, or if dollar signs flashed in his eyes. Big, fast bucks and the glare of media lights awaited him, if he wished.

When she slowly forced her gaze to meet his, she found that his expression hadn't changed much. He regarded her with the same solemn intensity that had underscored his question about her poetry. But the knowledge certainly glimmered in his stare—the truth and the lies.

"Hey!" cried the waitress, balancing a tray of dirty dishes beside their table and peering closely at Claire. "You look just like her. No kidding, you really do!"

The men at the dining counter swiveled around to gape, and families at surrounding tables craned their necks to see her. She heard a few murmurs, "Yeah, she does.... Just like her."

"You're even wearing sunglasses like she was," noted the waitress, "and carrying the same purse."

Claire stiffened with alarm. A false smile settled on her lips as she frantically searched for a reply. Her hand, already held by Walker, now gripped his in a painful squeeze.

She heard him laugh—a booming, jovial laugh that she knew to be as false as her own smile, though he pulled it off remarkably well. "How 'bout that, honey? They think you look like that Perfume Princess on the news!" In the same loud, husbandly tone he'd used at the airport, he addressed the room at large. "I hope this doesn't go to her head. Yesterday someone told her she sounded like Barbra Streisand, and I had to listen to her belting out 'People Who Need People' all night. Who knows what she'll be doing now?"

Chuckles sounded from around the room. The cook behind the counter muttered something about *his* wife thinking she was Gladys Knight and wanting him to be her Pip. The waitress shook her head with a smile, but continued to scrutinize Claire.

Though her tongue felt heavy and her body disjointed, Claire drew on her many years of training in the public eye. "Oh, go on, Jim. You liked my singing just as well as Barbra's. And maybe I never mentioned it during our twelve years of marriage, but I *am* that Perfume Princess." Widening her smile, Claire cocked her head toward Walker and said to the waitress, "Take this peasant to the dungeon, will ya, hon?"

The group around them broke into laughter and hooted.

Walker stood with an exaggerated grimace and dropped a few bills on the table. "I better get her out of here before she starts thinking about buying one of those yachts. C'mon, Suzanne."

"That's 'Your Highness' to you," she corrected with exaggerated arrogance. More laughs rang out. She rose on shaky legs, grateful for the supporting arm he wrapped around her.

Teasing comments followed them to the door.

"Make him bow, Suzanne!"

"Make him buy you one of them châteaus in the south of France!"

"*Then* throw him in the dungeon!"

The door closed on the crowd's lively hilarity.

Claire wasn't sure her legs would hold out all the way to the car. He half carried her the last few steps, then smoothly deposited her into the passenger seat. Taking his place behind the wheel, he started up the car and threw her a staid glance. "Breathe."

She did as he said—sucked a huge gulp of breath into her lungs, and then exhaled it.

"Again," he instructed.

She struggled through the process again. Amazingly enough, her lungs gradually geared into automatic, and sensation trickled back into her arms, fingers and toes. The trembling, though, had moved from her legs to the rest of her body.

What if Walker hadn't been there? What if she'd been dependent on a taxi driver to make her getaway? The driver himself might have recognized her. She would have been trapped, embarrassed, thrown to the media wolves. Walker had acted quickly and effectively. Even if the worst had occurred and the crowd had identified her beyond a doubt, she felt sure Walker would have physically swept her up and bundled her out of there before the media could have reached them.

He was a very good man to have in her corner. But was he *really* in her corner now?

He drove in silence, just as he had earlier this morning. An odd reaction to discovering such shocking news. She wondered what thoughts his unreadable expression concealed. Was he trying to decide on the most profitable course of action? She didn't want to think that; didn't even want to suspect it. But she'd been betrayed by friends, servants, even family members who had sold stories and pictures of her to the media. She couldn't allow herself to expect better from anyone.

Somehow this doubt about Walker hurt more than the other betrayals themselves had.

He surprised her by turning down a sandy road toward the beach. Windswept dunes swelled around them—rolling hills of malt-colored sand and waving sea oats, driftwood and dried seashells. The sound of the surf grew louder, and when the sparkling Gulf came into view, Walker parked the car and got out.

She waited until she was sure her legs would carry her, then followed his footsteps in the sand. Had he gone to make a call on his cell phone? Would the media be descending on them in droves, and the tabloids waving five- or six-figure checks in his direction? No, she couldn't make herself believe he'd be like so many others in her life.

She stopped beside him as he stood on the crest of a sandy mound and gazed out to sea, his hands in his pockets, his ebony hair riffling in the gusty breeze. After a prolonged silence, he said, "You weren't going to tell me, were you?"

Her voice emerged as a rusty whisper. "No."

"You were just going to grab a taxi and let me find out who you were later."

"Yes."

The wind dusted them with hot gusts of sand and bright white heat radiated from the surrounding dunes. Gulls circled and squawked overhead. The sun glared from the east, the smell of the sea misted the air and the sky shifted in pretty patterns of blue and fluffy white.

He seemed to be angry. She hadn't expected that.

She pushed her sunglasses back on her head, wanting to face him one last time without the shaded barrier between them. "Walker, I'm sorry. When I lied about my identity, well...it was nothing personal."

"Nothing personal? Ah. I see." He shifted his gaze to her. "Are you saying you don't consider the things we did together *personal?*"

"No, of course not. I only meant—"

"Is it considered sport in your exalted circles to masquerade as someone else...in bed?"

She stared at him, mortified. He deserved a sound slap for the insult. But oddly enough, the sharp words didn't bother her nearly as much as they should have. Another man might have been gloating to think he'd bedded a celebrity, or eager to win her favor. Walker was simply and honestly pissed off. Not that she intended to allow the insult to go unanswered.

"Oh, yes, bed masquerades are all the rage," she answered coolly. "We heiresses slip out at night to dupe the locals. It's always so much fun to read about it in the tabloids whenever we're caught."

They faced off in tense silence.

"Is that what you were afraid I was going to do—sell some lurid blow-by-blow account of our night together?"

"Any account of our night together would be bad enough," she declared, anguished.

Tyce squared his jaw and looked away. He wasn't sure why he was so angry. He of all people knew her fear was legitimate. Hattie had hired him in hopes of getting just such a scoop. Claire's lie about her identity had been understandable. She really couldn't trust many people.

Especially not him. Even now, he was hiding the fact that he'd been hired by both Hattie and her uncle to report on her. His hidden agenda weighed heavily on his conscience. He couldn't tell her the truth, though, or she wouldn't accept his protection.

But he still couldn't stop the anger from gnawing at his insides. He'd wanted her to confide in him. Wanted her to turn to him for help. She hadn't. She planned to leave him, grab a taxi and ride away, without a backward glance. He'd meant nothing more to her than a casual romp to spice up her vacation...the "wild oats" she'd sworn to sow.

Why should that bother you? he asked himself. She was a damn good lay. An unexpected perk after a long day on the job.

"Let's not fight," she implored. Her gaze had lost its frostiness, and he felt a wrenching in his gut. "I'm so grateful to you for everything you've done for me, Walker. Like...back there, in the diner. I panicked. I felt so exposed. Thank you for getting me out of there."

He realized then, staring into the eyes that still

took his breath away, that his anger was only partially directed at her. A good deal of it had to do with the images he'd seen on the television screen. Although he'd known from the start that she was a billionaire celebrity, he'd somehow forgotten the opulence of her life-style. The gowns and jewels she wore cost more than most people's homes. The mansions, villas and châteaus she lived in would turn even the richest man's head. An army of servants awaited at each location around the globe to serve her and her jet-setting friends. The yacht he'd seen on the newscast—with elegant lounges, saunas and a full-scale gym—could rival any luxury cruise ship. Why the hell had he thought, even for a moment, that the time they'd spent together would affect her in any way at all?

She was slumming, enjoying a brief sojourn into the lives of common folk, just to help her appreciate the luxuries she'd come to take for granted. She'd fly back to her enchanted existence in a matter of days, he was sure. His anger meant so little in the grand scheme of things that he felt ridiculous for having shown it.

Forcing the anger aside, he said with all the graciousness he could muster, "I'm glad to have been of assistance." She gazed deeper into his eyes than he would have liked. Any deeper and he just might lose all perspective and kiss her. He couldn't let himself do that. Now that her identity was out in the open, even touching her unnecessarily would be out of the question. He was, officially, her bodyguard, as far as she knew. A hired employee. And she was, officially, a billionaire celebrity, light-years beyond his reach. Their game of make-believe was over. To divert his thoughts and reestablish the necessary level of civility between them, he uttered, "Good thing you didn't order caviar and cream cheese for breakfast."

She blinked. "I would have, but I didn't see it on the menu."

He bit his cheek to stifle a smirk. She really didn't get it, did she? He couldn't help a twinge of resentment for the life-style that placed her so far beyond his reach. In a cooler tone, he queried, "Anything else you're beginning to miss?"

"Lobster-stuffed mushrooms, I guess. The way my chef makes them." She fell silent, and as he turned his face into the sea breeze, she laid a hand on his arm. Reflexively he stiffened. He wasn't sure he could take her touching him. "I don't even know your whole name," she said in an oddly beseeching whisper.

"Tyce. Tyce Walker."

She pulled her hand away, and the corner of her mouth lifted in a troubled smile. Softly she repeated, "Tyce."

He squared his shoulders, sucked in a breath, and silently cursed her for looking vulnerable. He could swear she was tucking the name away in her heart, as if to savor it later. Since when had he grown so damn fanciful? He had to put an end to this madness. "My offer still stands. I'll drive you wherever you want to go."

The troubled look in her violet-blue eyes deepened. "Thank you. The nearest train station, I suppose." She turned to head for the car.

"You don't need to take a train," he called after her. "I said I'd drive you."

"Even if I want to go across country?" she asked over her shoulder, her curls a bright flurry in the sea-scented wind.

"Yes."

She halted and turned so quickly he nearly walked into her. "Why?" she demanded.

"In case you've forgotten, I've been hired to drive you and protect you." Another lie—he'd been hired to report on her. But he'd protect her with his life, if need be.

"That was before you knew who I was."

"What difference does that make?"

"Plenty. To me, at least." She searched his face with an intensity that brought to the forefront of his mind all the secrets he hid from her. "Can I trust you, Tyce?"

Her use of his first name surprised and warmed him. Her question annoyed him to hell and back. "What kind of question is that?"

"A serious one. Can I trust you to keep my whereabouts a secret and my private affairs private?"

A deep frustration welled up within him. *He couldn't make that promise.* "If I say you can trust me, does that mean you can? It's like asking a man if he's honest. If he's not, he's going to say he is, anyway. What good would it do if I got down on my knees and swore on a hundred bibles that I could be trusted?"

"If you say you can be trusted—" she said, sounding as if she were just now reaching an important conclusion "—and I mean you, Tyce Walker...then I'll believe you."

His lips pulled tight, and the anger he'd been holding at bay twisted into something almost painful. She was too trusting for her own good. "And if I don't say it?"

Her golden brows drew together. His back teeth gritted and locked. His gaze waged a battle with hers that neither of them thoroughly understood. She backed away first, but claimed victory with a simple pronouncement. "I'll trust you anyway."

She trudged off to the car. Tyce stood rooted to the spot, feeling as if he'd been blindsided.

THE HELICOPTER had been a stroke of genius. It would be overlooked by anyone on the beach as just another tourist copter taking vacationers up for a panoramic view of the coast. Even now, another helicopter hovered a few miles to their west, and small planes flew advertising banners above the beach. Couldn't ask for better cover than that.

The pilot, however, would have to be replaced. Twice now, he'd messed up a perfectly good shot with his unsteady flying.

"Hold this thing level, will ya?" Hattie yelled

to the pilot over the roar of the wind and the whirring of the propellers. She then turned to the balding, potbellied photographer who aimed a camera through the open door. "Zoom in on 'em now, Sam."

He clicked a few shots of T.K. and the Perfume Princess standing on a sand dune.

Hattie smiled, well pleased. Slick Sam was the only photographer she trusted to keep his mouth shut about a story as hot as this one. She'd given him good cause. She'd promised him stock in her tabloid. She might have even turned this scoop over to him entirely instead of bringing T.K. in on it, except that Sam had been down with the flu at the time.

The day she'd hired T.K. to tail Valentina, she'd poured a whole pot of chicken soup down Sam's throat, force-fed him antibiotics and kept a bed-pan beside him at all times in case he threw up. So far he hadn't. But if this pilot didn't hold the damn copter steady, Sam would be sure to hurl. Which would make them miss some good photo ops.

"Oh, hell, they're leaving." Nervously she shoved a cigarette in her mouth.

"What's the big deal?" croaked Sam, looking a little green as he fell heavily against his seat and set the telescopic camera aside. "We got plenty of pictures. How'd those ones turn out that you took from the cartridge of T.K.'s sunglasses?"

"Fine. Nothing real hot, though." Hattie lit her

cigarette. "Hey, pay attention, Frankie!" she shouted at the pilot. "Follow that car!"

"Think T.K. will take any more pictures?" Sam asked.

"Who knows? I put a fresh cartridge in, but he gets touchy about pictures, especially when the story has to do with her. Don't ask me why. Remember when he broke your telescopic lens before her debutante ball?"

"Yeah." Sam uttered a few choice curses. "Could have had some great cover shots."

"That's why I took the cartridge out of his sunglasses last night when I had the chance. The way they were looking at each other on the dance floor, I figured he'd change his mind about giving the photos to me. I'll bet he'd have kept 'em for himself."

"Wouldn't have made much difference. I got some great shots myself after you left." His double-chinned grin was the one Hattie loved—the one that meant they'd hit pay dirt. "You're gonna flip when you see 'em." Sam chuckled and shook his head. "That T.K....he's one lucky bastard."

"Hey!" Hattie backhanded him across the chest, sending Sam into a spasm of coughing. "Don't talk that way about my kid."

"Oh, sorry. Didn't mean no disrespect. By the way..." The look that came over Sam's rotund face now made the hairs stand up on Hattie's arms. *Greed.* She hadn't expected to see it on Sam's face anytime soon. Hadn't she promised him enough to buy his loyalty? "I've been offered twice as much for these photos as what you're willing to pay. Even including the stock in the tabloid."

She glared at him. If her hands hadn't grown unsteady and her eyes too weak, she would have taken her own pictures. She hated getting old. "Are you telling me you put those pictures up for bid?"

"I just asked around, that's all."

"Asked around! Are you crazy? By now, word is out that we've got something hot. How long do you think it'll take for everyone and his brother to move in on us? We've probably led 'em right to her."

"You're missing the point, Hattie. With the pictures I've got, I can retire." That double-chinned grin split his face again. "As a multimillionaire."

Hattie took a long, hard drag on her cigarette, then blew the smoke out in steady white streams from her nose. "No, *you're* missing the point, Sammy. Those pictures are mine. And if they should find their way to another paper, I have a few photos of my own that your sweet little wife might be interested in seeing. Took 'em back in January. A hotel outside of London."

The light of greed in Sam's eyes extinguished, and that sickly green pallor returned. "You wouldn't."

"'Course not." She might be getting old, but she hadn't forgotten the importance of good management techniques. "I wouldn't do a thing like that to my *partner*, now...would I?"

7

"LET'S HEAD FOR DALLAS. The woman who raised me—Nanny, I used to call her—told me it's a wonderful place. She has family there. I wonder if they'd still remember me? I met some of her grandchildren at Christmas one year…" She must have realized he was only partially listening to this American princess he'd been calling "Claire," the one who stubbornly insisted on trusting him. She fell silent, then asked, "Is something wrong?"

He didn't want to worry her, but he saw no way around it. "It's possible that we're being followed."

"Followed!" She whipped around in her seat to look behind them. "Here, in the sand dunes?"

Tyce nodded grimly and gazed through the rearview mirror as he drove down the sandy path between the dunes. He understood the doubt in her voice. They seemed to be very much alone.

"I don't see anyone," she ventured, both anxious and hopeful.

"That helicopter back there, over the water."

"The helicopter? Oh!" She breathed a sigh of relief. "That's only one of those tourist rides. I saw a couple of them when we first got here, and believe me, I almost hit the floor to hide, but then I realized what they were. Hadn't you noticed them flying up and down the beach yesterday?"

Yesterday. Had it only been yesterday? Their day on the beach seemed a lifetime ago. She'd been masquerading as an ordinary vacationer, and though he'd known she wasn't, he'd taken her playacting a little too seriously. He wished the truth hadn't come out in the open. It sat between them like an unscalable wall, at least for him. "Yeah, I noticed the copters yesterday. This one *could* be a tourist ride, and the passengers *could* be looking through binoculars at the panoramic view...but I don't like the way it circled back around to us."

Like a candle snuffed out, the relief vanished from her face, and she looked skyward through her passenger window.

Tyce silently cursed himself for the hundredth time in the short few days he'd been with her. He should have spotted the copter sooner. He'd been too caught up in her to pay much attention to the sky around them. Subconsciously he must have noticed, though, because a feeling of unease had grown in the pit of his stomach. By the time he'd ushered her to the car, he'd known something wasn't quite right, and had searched around him for a clue to his unease.

"The helicopter *is* following us!" she cried as he steered the car onto the paved highway. "It's paparazzi...isn't it?"

It wasn't really a question. She knew as well as he did. "I believe so."

She shut her eyes and leaned her head back. "They found me *again*. We can't shake them, can we?" Her voice shook with disappointment. "The whole elaborate plan, the risk, all for nothing. It's over."

"Hey, it's *not* over. We'll lose 'em."

"No, we won't." Her eyes opened, and they were glazed with a hunted look. "I can't get away from them."

"Claire." He reached an arm around her and pulled her to him. She was his "Claire" right now, the woman he'd held and kissed last night, not the heiress on the television screen. He wished he could stop the car to hold her closer. "Don't throw in the towel yet," he said against her temple. "They're too far away to do anything right now, and we're going to lose them."

She shook her head. "They're everywhere." In a tight whisper, she added, "Even when I close my eyes, I see them."

"I'll keep them away." A brash promise, he knew, but one he'd try his best to keep. Holding her tightly with one arm, he kept a hand on the wheel and his eyes on the road.

Silent now, she let herself rest against him. After a moment, she pulled away and settled in her own seat. She was, once again, the princess. But when she turned her pale, heart-shaped face his way, he saw anger simmering there. "They force their way into the most private parts of my life, until I *don't* have a private life at all."

Her fervent words shamed him for having worked in the profession that preyed on her. He wanted to bear down on the accelerator and tear around the other cars, but it wouldn't be smart to let the paparazzi know they'd been spotted. They'd only follow more closely, more blatantly. Better to pretend he was unaware of their presence and lose them with a decoy.

Fred and the small, handpicked crew he'd summoned earlier that morning should have arrived by now in Panama City. He'd call them, but not on the cell phone, or the conversation could be picked up on a scanner. He'd have to stop at a phone booth, an inside one where the paparazzi couldn't see him making the call.

"How could they have found us?" she wondered, sounding anguished. "We were so careful."

"I don't know." His first guess was Hattie. He should have known better than to trust her promise not to keep him under surveillance, or her claim that legal battles would be keeping her in the office. "Don't worry—we're going to lose them."

He blended smoothly into the flow of traffic on the highway, taking care not to pass too many cars or look as if he were in any particular hurry. His mind, however, raced. If Hattie was following him now, she probably had been keeping track of his location electronically from the outset.

She could have used tags on the car he'd rented, his luggage, his cell phone—hell, just about anything, since she probably had access to his apartment before he'd left. He doubted he'd been tailed in person until now, but he had to admit, he could have overlooked someone in the crowded bar last night.

He recalled Claire "losing" the sunglasses he'd given her, the ones with a microcamera in the frame. He'd bet a small fortune that they'd been stolen from her purse at the bar. Again, he suspected Hattie. She knew about the camera in the sunglasses and would have found the opportunity irresistible to steal the photos he'd already taken of Claire. Memory flashed of the guy in the Hawaiian shirt this morning who'd pushed rudely past them in the condo hallway, right before they'd found the sunglasses. He could have planted them there. Hattie would have wanted to return the sunglasses, undoubtedly with a fresh cartridge, so he could take more pictures.

Good thing for Hattie that she was out of reach. He would have cherished the opportunity to strangle her. The idea of having those photos published—photos he himself had taken of Claire—suddenly seemed like an unforgivable betrayal. He wished he'd never taken them. Ironically enough, he'd decided last night to keep the photos for himself, a memento of his time with her. He realized now that mere photos, or any memento, would never be enough.

"The copter's still following us, isn't it?"

"Yeah. Keep your face covered," he advised. "They can't sell pictures as easily if you're not identifiable in them."

She tugged her sun hat low over her face and slouched down in the seat. He hated that she had to ride with a hat over her face. He hated even more all the secrets he hid from her. Like the fact that he'd taken photos of her that would probably end up in a tabloid. At least the photos were innocent beach shots that could have been taken by anybody. But Hattie or whoever was following them would have other photos by now. He could just imagine the camera shutters whirring last night at the bar. And afterward.

Foreboding curled like talons in his chest. Exactly which of many possible candid poses would be immortalized?

"If paparazzi are following us now," he reasoned out aloud, his throat tight with dismay, "they may have been yesterday, too."

"Yesterday? You mean, on the beach?"

"And…afterward."

Once again, the color drained alarmingly from her face. She knew, of course, what he meant. Their time in the bar, on the dance floor, and on their way to the condo. Worse yet, in the corridor outside the condo, wrapped in each other's arms. He hadn't seen anybody around them, but at the time he might not have noticed a Sherman tank in the corridor.

How had he lost his head so completely? He'd disregarded all the rules he'd ever set for himself, including every shred of common sense. He deserved to be shot, dragged through the streets in shackles, drawn and quartered, thrown to the wolves.

He probably would be, he realized, if certain photos hit the papers and his powerful client, her uncle, saw them. That prospect didn't bother him nearly as much as the chance that Claire would discover his role in procuring the photos.

He pulled into a gas station and parked. "Lie down on the seat, as if you're sleeping. Keep your head covered and the doors locked. I'll be right back."

"Be careful, Tyce. If they know you're with me, you'll be a target, too."

He had to admit, he hadn't thought of that. She was right, though. If certain photos taken last night hit the papers, his face would become internationally famous by tomorrow morning, if not sooner. The paparazzi would be thick on his tail.

Ironic.

And if the news got out that he'd been working for a tabloid, how much faith would clients put in his discretion as a private investigator and security expert?

He put on his sunglasses, locked the car doors and hurried to an inside phone. While he waited for Fred to answer, he turned toward the wall, took off his glasses and searched them for electronic tracking devices. He found none. He then opened the microcamera within their frame. The cartridge was there, but that meant nothing. Hat-

tie would have replaced it with a new one. Dropping the tiny cartridge to the floor, he ground it
beneath his heel, picked it up and tossed it into a
nearby trash can. He then instructed Fred on
where to meet him, who to bring along and how
to proceed.

Before returning to the car, he stopped at the
small convenience store within the gas station
and bought two oversize Florida State Seminoles
T-shirts and baseball caps. When he returned to
the car, he opened her passenger door and
handed her a shirt and cap. "Get out, put these
on, then walk over to that vending machine. I
want our friends in the sky to get a good look at
us dressed this way."

"Get out? You think I should get out of the car?
But they'll see me putting it on. What good will a
disguise do if they—"

"You said you trusted me, didn't you?"

"Well, yes, but—"

"Then just do it."

Tight-lipped and white-faced, she climbed out
of the car, stood beside it in clear view of the helicopter that now hovered a discreet distance away,
and pulled on the large garnet-and-gold T-shirt,
careful not to dislodge her sunglasses. She then
placed the billed cap on her head.

"Push all your hair up into the cap," he ordered, keeping his voice quiet so the customers at
the nearby gas pumps wouldn't hear. He donned
the other T-shirt and cap, then warned, "Don't

look at the copter. We don't want them to know we've spotted them."

"I don't understand why you want them to see us wearing—"

"You'll understand soon enough."

As they drove down the highway headed east toward Tallahassee, he explained the plan. He'd arranged for a man and woman to meet them at a roadside rest area, where they'd swap vehicles and make a getaway.

Claire's anxiety mounted. "These people we're meeting…how do you know they can be trusted?"

"They've worked for me for years. They're some of the best security agents in the business."

"They work for you?" For some reason, this surprised her. She'd been thinking of him as a loner, a maverick, working entirely on his own.

"Yeah, and they're good. So don't worry, okay?"

She didn't argue, or point out to him that she'd been betrayed by people she'd trusted implicitly. What good would it do? She had to trust somebody. She'd decided that somebody would be Tyce. She refused to second-guess him.

Only a pickup and a semi were parked in the neat, paved lot beside a sunny picnic area with tables and grills. The helicopter, Claire noticed, now hovered a mile or so behind them over the rural interstate. It could have been mistaken for a traffic copter, but Claire knew better. It was paparazzi. She felt it in her bones.

A deep anger resonated inside of her. They had no right to stalk her like this. She wished she could snatch them out of the sky and shake some sense of decency into them. She had no doubt they were snapping pictures of her and Tyce as they walked from the car to the small building that contained the water fountains and rest rooms. She kept her head down and her sunglasses on.

Once they were inside, she headed directly for the ladies' room and into a stall. Just as he'd predicted, a woman of about her height and build stood at the sink, apparently brushing her short, dark hair. The woman soon stepped into the stall beside hers and whispered, "Here, take these."

Claire looked down and saw the woman's hand extended beneath the partition, holding the glossy brown wig and flowered cotton dress she'd been wearing. Claire took them and handed over her T-shirt and cap. Although they were alone in the rest room, neither of them spoke. The woman next handed her a pair of white plastic sunglasses and seashell earrings. Claire gave her the sunglasses and earrings she'd been wearing.

She remembered that Tyce had instructed her to wait in the rest room a full ten minutes after her decoy had left it. She remained where she was, hidden in the stall, while the woman now wearing the Seminoles cap emerged from the stall beside her. Over the top of the door, Claire watched her leave the rest room. Her heart pounded as she waited out the full ten minutes, checking her watch at half-minute intervals that felt like for-ever.

When the time came she stepped out of the stall, adjusted the bobbed, chin-length wig in the mirror and tied the sash of the simple cotton dress that was only slightly too large for her.

Taking a deep breath, she left the rest room, re-membering vividly the last time she'd donned a disguise in a public rest room and headed out for freedom. Her escape then had been caught on videotape and broadcast to the world. She was still chasing that freedom, and more desperate than ever to find it. She'd had a taste—a brief, wonderful taste—and craved more.

When a man in a light denim shirt, sleek black sunglasses and a tan Stetson took hold of her arm, she almost jerked away from him in fright. Silly of her. Tyce had told her to expect him in a cowboy hat. She forced a smile and accompanied him to the car. To the truck, actually. A shiny, black pickup with enormous wheels and heavily tinted windows.

The gray sedan they'd been in had already left. She didn't dare look up to see if the helicopter had followed it, but she listened for its distant thrumming sound and heard nothing over the hammering of her own heart.

The only other vehicles in the lot were the semi in the far corner and a motorcycle parked beside them. The sight of the motorcycle, even without its rider, gave her a start. Paparazzi in Europe often favored motorcycles. Not so much here, though. But one could never be sure....

Tyce swept her smoothly past the motorcycle and helped her up onto the high bench seat of the pickup. She sat stiffly and twisted her hands in her lap as he started the rumbling truck engine, backed out of the parking space and drove away from the rest area. The motorcycle remained where it was, thank God, with its rider nowhere in sight.

As they motored down the expressway in the opposite direction from where they'd been headed, she realized she'd been holding her breath. Slowly she exhaled. "Is the copter gone?" She couldn't bring herself to look.

He exited the expressway and turned north onto a two-lane country road. Slanting her a smile, he pushed the Stetson back on his head with an easy gesture she recognized from cowboy movies. "Took off after Fred and Wanda like hounds chasing a rabbit."

Hardly daring to believe, she checked behind them herself—both the sky and the road. No one, not a single vehicle, was in sight.

Gladness fizzled through her like fine champagne, making her feel light-headed and lighthearted. "We did it! We lost them!" Tossing her sunglasses aside, she scooted across the seat and looped her arms around his neck. "*You* lost them. You're a genius, Tyce Walker. And my hero."

"Aw, shucks, ma'am," he drawled, dipping his head in a show of modesty that would do any cowboy proud, his lazy smile deepening the vertical crease beside his mouth.

She laughed, plucked the interfering sunglasses from his face and planted an exuberant smooch on his lean, angled cheek, right where the lightning-white scar crossed it.

"Whoa! Hold on thar, little lady." Without taking his eyes from the road, he reached up with one hand to tilt his hat back to its proper angle. "What in tarnation do you think you're—"

His western drawl broke off as she planted another loud kiss just below the laugh lines of his eye...then a softer one near the strong, clean line of his jaw. His smile went a little off kilter. She pulled back, just far enough to catch the troubled surprise in his glance, then dropped a kiss below his ear.

An unsteady rush of breath escaped him, and he slanted his face to force the next kiss nearer to his mouth. This one stirred her senses with the taste of him, the scent of him. He stopped her with the look in his forest-dark eyes, too intense to be playful. "Claire," he whispered gruffly, "don't kiss me unless you mean it."

Her blood warmed, her eyes closed, and she pressed her lips to the corner of his mouth, meaning it with all her heart.

He groaned, his arm came up around her and he steered the truck to the side of the road, off onto a graveled shoulder beneath a canopy of oaks. He shut off the engine, threw the gearshift forward and turned to her, his gaze heated and intense.

He kissed her with a slow, undulating thoroughness that pressed her back against the seat and sent shards of heat through her. His hand swept up the length of her throat, his fingers curved around her jaw and he angled his kiss deeper. She opened wider, coaxing him in. She couldn't get enough of him this way, though, not nearly enough. And from his frustrated moans, it seemed he couldn't get enough of her.

When the longing grew to a near-violent pitch, he broke off and rested his forehead against hers. "Let's go somewhere we can be alone," he said, his breathing hard.

She nodded, wanting that fiercely. Wondering if it were really possible. *Trust in him*, she told herself. He'd shaken off the paparazzi, hadn't he?

He stole one last, sweet, lingering kiss, brushed the backs of his fingers down the curve of her face and smiled into her eyes with a tenderness that wrapped around her heart. Then he turned from her and repositioned himself behind the wheel. But as he reached for the key in the ignition, he froze.

"Tyce?"

"Shh. Listen."

She heard it then. An almost inaudible ticking sound, coming from somewhere beneath the truck. She frowned. "What is it?"

His face had paled beneath his tan. "Open your door," he ordered in a curiously strained, deadpan tone. "Get out of the truck and walk into the woods." His hand reached for his own door handle. "*Far* into the woods."

"You want me to—"

"Do it now!" he growled, frightening her into action. She fumbled for her door handle, shoved the heavy truck door open and fell out into the roadside brush. Her legs and dress tangled in sharp, thorny weeds as she struggled to stand.

She'd taken no more than half a dozen staggering steps when the world exploded around her. A deafening roar, a blinding flash, a push of fiery heat against her back, kicking her forward, pitching her headlong into a blur.

And searing pain.

Confusion.

Blackness.

8

SHE HEARD more than saw the people around her, although a blur of faces and hands imposed itself on her now and then. The voices were clear enough most of the time. She understood much of what they said, the ones who spoke directly to her, but it was *his* voice she clung to, *his* face she focused on, during those flashes of clarity.

It was important to see him, to hear him. More important than anything.

She'd been hurt, it seemed, but she felt no pain. He told her she'd be all right. He was carrying her. Odd, that he'd be carrying her. He was taking her to a safe place, he said. It sounded nice. *A safe place.* She felt safe now, as if wrapped in a comfortable cocoon and watching a hubbub of activity that had little to do with her.

"Your name," another man was asking her. "Do you know your name?"

A curious little jab of reluctance disturbed her. She knew her name. Claire. But there were other names, too, and she didn't want to think about them, or talk about them.

"Don't ask her that," she heard Tyce say. "She's lucid. She called my name when she first opened her eyes."

A woman's face swam before her. The woman looked vaguely familiar. Something about a rest room stall and a baseball cap. "Do you know where you are, Claire?"

"Yes." She knew where she was. In a way.

"Where? Where are you?"

Again, the reluctance, the disturbing reluctance to answer. "Ask Tyce," she replied. "Tyce Walker. Ask him. He knows."

She thought she heard his brief laugh, and it comforted her.

The voices grew distant, and a roaring in her ears grew louder. She let the sound wash over her, pretending it was the sea. The sound of the surf rolling onto the shore. It wasn't, she knew. It was too loud to be the sea.

"A jet," he was telling her. "I'm taking you on a private jet, Claire. There's a nurse here who's coming with us."

It tired her, trying to make sense of it, and she let her eyes drift shut.

"No, stay awake. Open your eyes, Claire. Talk to me."

Nice, that he wanted her to talk to him. She loved talking to him. She loved the way he listened, as if every word was important, even when it wasn't important at all. She loved the way he'd frown at her, or smile. Or sometimes yell. He made her feel very real, somehow.

"Your favorite breakfast, Claire. What do you like for breakfast?"

"Caviar," she roused herself enough to answer, "and cream cheese."

"What else?"

"Canadian bacon."

They were lifting her, many hands, and then they were lowering her. Laying her down on something soft. But he wasn't holding her anymore, and she didn't like it. "Tyce?" She lifted an arm and found that it was heavy, too heavy, but she couldn't let it drop back down until she found him.

"I'm here." His voice sounded hoarse, gruff. His face hovered above her, so dearly familiar, but somber and intense. "I'm right here. I won't leave you. The nurse wants you to stay awake. What else do you like for breakfast? Some kind of sauce?"

Cute, that he wanted to know. She smiled and slipped into a cozy darkness. His voice droned on, urging her to do this, do that, answer this, answer that. She wanted to cooperate. She really did. But it was too much of a strain to focus on his requests when she was so very, very tired.

And cold. Trembling cold. He uttered something that sounded urgent. Blankets wrapped around her. The darkness deepened. At its edges, shadow phantoms pressed in. Sinister phantoms, creeping up on her. She groaned.

A strong, warm hand touched her—held her hand, stroked her face. She found his voice again. His gruff, insistent voice. Relief washed through her. His voice, his touch, warmed the darkness and kept the phantoms away.

She slept.

HE RETURNED to the cabin just as the sun rose above the rolling green terrain of eastern Ohio, its early morning rays barely strong enough yet to dilute the darkness. He ached with tension and his eyes burned from lack of sleep as he pushed open the log cabin's front door.

Brianna Rowland, the elegant young wife of one of his favorite business associates, looked up at him with a gentle smile as she set a plate of biscuits and smoky sausage links on his kitchen table. Tyce sent up a silent prayer of thanks that she'd come, that she'd left her own family yesterday afternoon and stayed all night with the doctor and Claire while he himself had been busy setting up a perimeter guard and issuing orders for his investigators. Both Brianna and the physician, Doctor Noreen Myers, would keep this matter of an injured runaway heiress strictly confidential, he knew. A tall order for most people.

"It's about time you're back. You've been out all night." And though Brianna herself had been up all night, too, every strand of her light brown hair remained neatly twined in a smooth twist, small gold studs glinted at her ears and her beige slacks outfit looked as fresh as when she'd arrived yesterday. "Come sit down and have breakfast," she ordered in her firm yet soft-spoken way that somehow always garnered cooperation.

At the moment, however, Tyce couldn't bring himself to sit or eat. His gaze went to the closed bedroom door on the far left of the massive stone fireplace. "Is she all right?" He hardly recognized the raw, weary voice as his own.

"No change in her condition since the last time you asked," drawled Dr. Myers from another corner of the kitchen, coffeepot in hand, her brown eyes gleaming in her warm, dark face as she regarded Tyce with wry exasperation, "which was about three minutes ago."

"No, the last time he called us from his walkie-talkie was—" Brianna checked her watch "—at least eight minutes ago, Doc."

Tyce acknowledged their teasing with a weary half smile, relieved that they *were* teasing rather than delivering bad news. He supposed he *had* called from his walkie-talkie quite a few times while stationing his men around the property. He couldn't help it. His worry about Claire interfered with every breath, every heartbeat. He wouldn't have left her side if the need hadn't been so great to post guards at strategic points and to set the rest of his staff into motion on finding the would-be murderer.

The thought of someone actually trying to kill Claire washed over him again with icy dread. He'd snatched her out of death's fiery jaws by mere seconds. Fierce anger still shook him. He'd find the son of a bitch who'd planted that bomb and kill him himself, if he had to.

"She's sleeping peacefully," Brianna assured

him as he continued toward the bedroom. "We woke her again a few minutes ago, and she's fine. Come eat."

"And then you can take a pain pill," Noreen advised. "The cut on your arm probably should have had stitches, and that ankle of yours was swollen pretty badly yesterday. I can imagine what it looks like now. You're limping."

"I'm fine," he murmured on his way to the bedroom. It wasn't exactly true. His ankle hurt like hell, but he didn't want to fog his mental state with any kind of medication. He had to stay alert to protect Claire.

Quietly he paced into the bedroom and peered at the woman asleep in his bed. She was so damn beautiful. Just looking at her made him ache in ways he'd never ached before. And just thinking about the possibility of permanent injuries to her turned him sick and cold.

He'd had to make a tough decision yesterday— to take her to a Florida hospital, which could have exposed her to the bomber again, or fly her to safety, which could have worsened her medical condition. His crew, whom he summoned from a phone at a nearby farmhouse, had come to his aid by finding a nurse to fly with them on the jet. He'd sent the woman back to Florida generously rewarded. He only hoped she hadn't recognized her famous patient—or wouldn't talk about it if she had.

Thankful that Claire seemed to have come through the ordeal intact, he reluctantly returned to his guests, who now sat with coffee and sausage biscuits in his kitchen.

"I take it that by now, you have the whole mountain surrounded by armed guards," remarked Noreen, the tall, stately physician with cocoa-brown skin and only a few glints of silver in her short, ebony curls.

Tyce nodded, sat and took the steaming mug she handed him. Brianna fixed him a plate of food. He realized then that they, along with Brianna's husband, Jake, were probably the closest he'd had to friends since Joe had been sent to prison. Until now, he'd always considered them business acquaintances. He'd handled investigations for them, and Jake had advised him on investments. There were few people he trusted more.

Right now, he even had doubts about a couple of his own security agents. Someone had planted a bomb in the pickup. The only way they would have known about that pickup was if his crew had been followed, their actions monitored and their conversations overheard.

Tyce vowed to find out how and who. He'd take nothing for granted.

He wouldn't even trust her uncle, the man who'd hired him to follow her, or anyone else in her family. Though he hadn't asked her yet about the terms of her will, he suspected her family figured prominently in it. A fortune such as hers could be one powerful motivation to kill.

Even if her uncle was innocent, the bomber

could have found Claire through Tyce's contact with him. If word had leaked out about his hiring Tyce to find her, a clever and determined nutcase could have tracked Claire through the investigators who'd been working for him. Tyce and his crew might have unwittingly led some psychopath to her. He'd make no more reports to her uncle until the would-be assassin was in custody.

He forced himself to eat, his mind roiling with half-formed plans, concerns and questions.

"Tyce, why don't you go get some sleep?" Brianna suggested, always the mother hen, though she was probably younger than him. "You look exhausted. Valentina might need you later."

He couldn't argue with that. With an absent nod, he headed toward his bedroom.

"Uh, Tyce." Brianna lifted a tawny brow. "You might want to use another bedroom. Our patient is sleeping in that one."

He paused with his hand on the bedroom doorknob. Only then did he realize the absurdity of what he'd almost done. He'd been about to lie down in bed with Valentina Richmond as if he had every right to do so. It probably would have humiliated her, being wakened by Noreen or Brianna at the next hourly interval to find her bodyguard in bed with her.

Her bodyguard.

What had started out as a ruse had become fact. He'd taken the task upon himself without anyone hiring him to do so. His top priority—his *only* priority—was to protect Claire.

But that certainly didn't give him any personal claim on her. What the hell had he been thinking, heading for her bed? With a disgusted shake of his head, he veered off toward one of the guest bedrooms.

He hadn't been thinking at all. He'd simply wanted to hold her.

BRIGHT SUNLIGHT PRIED Claire's eyes open, and she found herself in a log cabin of some sort. A ski chalet, maybe. Had she been skiing? She sat up against the pillows and pain shot through her head. Pain! She'd been hurt.

She probably *had* been skiing.

But then memory filtered back to her in strange bits and pieces—standing on a beach, riding in a car, running from someone. A helicopter. Paparazzi. An explosion. Tyce!

Her head spun with worry, questions and pain. Had she seen him after that, or had she been dreaming? The memories seemed so foggy and unreal. She looked around with growing panic, finding only a woman in the room with her. A stranger, seated in an armchair beside the bed. Fear pumped through Claire. "Where's Tyce Walker?"

The woman glanced her way and set aside a sheaf of papers she'd been reading, her hazel eyes meeting hers with warmth and reassurance. "He's here. We talked him into getting some sleep. He was up all night, arranging for your protection." Slim and attractive in beige slacks and top, her tawny hair drawn up in a twist, the woman smiled. "I'm glad to see you're awake. We were worried. How do you feel?"

Claire sat up higher against the pillows, feeling achy and bruised all over. "Like I've been run over by a truck."

"I wouldn't doubt that. You're probably exhausted, too. Dr. Myers insisted we wake you every couple hours last night."

She tried to remember. Slowly it came back— hazy recollections of being wakened and forced to answer a trite question or two. "A doctor was here?"

"She still is. She's on the phone with her office at the moment. For security reasons, Tyce refused to take you to a hospital, but he had Dr. Myers waiting here when you arrived. She's an excellent physician, and a good friend of ours."

A good friend of ours. Had she been speaking of Tyce and her? Who was she to him?

"By the way, I'm Brianna Rowland." She extended her hand for a businesslike shake. "I'm glad to meet you, Ms. Richmond."

Disappointed to be called by her real name, Claire politely shook the woman's hand. She wasn't ready to go back to reality yet. And she wasn't at all sure that this Brianna Rowland or the doctor she'd mentioned could be trusted to keep her identity a secret. "Please, call me Claire."

Brianna inclined her head in gracious agreement.

"What happened?" Claire asked. "I remember an explosion. What was it?"

Dismay flickered in Brianna's eyes. "The truck you'd been riding in exploded."

"Was it a bomb?" Her insides clenched with anxiety at the very possibility.

"The police believe it was. Tyce is sending his own investigators to find out more."

Her anxiety deepened into fear. They'd almost been killed, Tyce and she. Intentionally. By whom? The stalker? The thought of someone being so twisted and obsessed terrified her.

Brianna reached across the rumpled blankets and laid a hand over hers. "Don't worry. You're safe here, Claire. Tyce will make sure of that."

The woman's gentle touch helped calm her. "Has Tyce been hurt?"

"If so, he won't admit it. Too macho, you know." Her eyes sparkled with rueful fondness.

Claire hoped fervently that this Brianna wasn't romantically involved with Tyce. She wanted to like her. The possibility that she *was* involved with him hurt far more than any of her physical pains. Why should that be? She should be thinking of her grave situation—not wondering whether this woman was Tyce's lover. Forcing her thoughts back on track, she asked, "Has the media picked up on the explosion?"

"It was mentioned briefly on the news last night, but only as an unexplained vehicle fire. No one, not even the police, knows you were involved. Tyce said he carried you away from the scene before they got there."

Claire wondered how long it would take for the media to put the puzzle together. If the paparazzi had found her at the beach, she didn't doubt they'd connect her with the vehicle bombing. The search for her would intensify mercilessly then. Her cousin would worry that she'd been killed, seriously hurt or kidnapped. She wished she could call him, just to assure him she was okay.

Looking around the spacious, log-walled bedroom, Claire asked, "Where are we?"

"Tyce's house. His summer cabin, actually."

Another surprise. He'd brought her to his place. The idea warmed her. Then again, if this was Tyce's place, why was Brianna acting as her hostess? Maybe it would be better not to know.

"Are we in Florida?" Claire queried. "Georgia?"

"Ohio."

"Ohio!"

Brianna smiled at her surprise. "You might not remember very clearly, but he brought you here by jet yesterday. We're surrounded by forest and Amish farmland. The closest town is a forty-minute drive, and it's so small I'm sure you've never heard of it. Tyce likes the isolation. I think that's the main reason he bought this house and land, even though he spends most of the year elsewhere."

He spends most of the year elsewhere, she'd

said. Not *we*. That much was encouraging. Claire then noticed the gold-and-diamond ring on Brianna's left hand. Her heart gave a sudden, painful lurch. Surely she couldn't be Tyce's *wife*?

"You're married?" croaked Claire.

"Very," she replied with a grin. "If you stay here for a while, you'll probably meet my husband, Jake, and our daughter. We live a few miles up the river."

The relief was almost painful. Brianna was happily married to someone else. Why in heaven's name should that matter? But it did, she realized. It mattered too much. "I'd love to meet your family," Claire replied with much more warmth than she'd shown earlier. A sudden worry occurred to her. "But I wouldn't want to endanger them, or you. I mean, if someone is targeting me…"

"Tyce will find them, whoever they are," stated a mellow-rich feminine voice from the doorway. Dressed in a navy blazer, slacks and a white blouse, a handsome woman with smooth, dark brown skin strolled into the room. The stethoscope around her neck, the blood-pressure kit in her hand, and an air of unmistakable authority proclaimed her profession. "I'm Dr. Myers, and I can promise you one thing. If anyone can keep you safe and hunt down the bad guys, it's Tyce Walker. Now hold up your arm so I can check your blood pressure."

Claire did as she was told, worrying even more about Tyce. She'd known he was protecting her, of course, but hadn't expected him to actively "hunt down the bad guys." The danger he'd be putting himself in made her feel sick with anxiety.

"Tyce said you're traveling incognito. I'm not sure whether to call you Ms. Jones or Ms. Richmond. Which would you prefer?" Dr. Myers raised her brows questioningly as she pumped up a band that grew taut around Claire's arm and monitored the results.

"I'd rather you call me Claire."

The doctor removed the pressure band. "Then I'd rather you call me Noreen."

Claire felt truly honored. She didn't think many people who weren't personal friends would be granted the right to address this woman as anything other than "Doctor."

"Put your mind at ease, Claire. You hired the right man." Noreen sat on the edge of the bed and flashed a small light into her eyes. "When things seem their worst, Tyce Walker has a way of setting them right. That's how I met him, you know. I hired him to clear my son's name."

"Your son?"

Noreen clicked off her little penlight. "He'd run off to New York City to make a name for himself with his music. Only nineteen, not even out of college yet, and thinking he had a chance to break into the big time. He broke into the big time, all right. The 'big house.' New York State Penitentiary." Her voice lowered. "They said he robbed a store at gunpoint. He was convicted of armed robbery."

Claire's heart went out to her. Though her tone was still light, her lips had tightened and her eyes dulled with bleak remembrances.

"I'm a widow, a single mother. I had to leave my practice here—my only income—and travel to New York. I spent two years and every dime of my savings hiring defense lawyers. The police had no evidence against him. The store owner himself didn't even identify him beyond a doubt. All they had was hearsay—from the local street gang that terrorized the neighborhood. But it was enough." Noreen's pained gaze focused on Claire. "My boy's not like that. He doesn't steal or rob, and he doesn't hold with any kind of violence. He didn't deserve to be locked away in prison with the scum of the earth who—" Her voice wavered and broke off. She looked away, sucked in a sharp breath. After a moment, she forced a tight smile. "I heard about Tyce from another mother who'd come to visit her son at the prison. By that time I had no money. Not even credit left to my name. But I was desperate, so I called him." She shook her head, as if she still couldn't believe it. "He investigated the case. Rounded up the so-called witnesses, interviewed the store owner, dug up evidence the police had overlooked. Then he put up his own money for a high-priced attorney to reopen the case." A fine sheen coated her eyes, and her nostrils flared. "He got my boy off. Brought him home to me."

No one said a word. Claire's chest was too tight for her to speak. It hurt to think that injustices like that happened. It made her glad, fiercely glad, that Tyce had cared enough to set things right.

"He investigated a case for my husband, too," Brianna quietly informed her from the armchair. "Got his brother released from an embezzlement charge. Found the woman who did it and brought back the money."

"Oh, my," Claire finally uttered. "And I hadn't even realized he handled investigations. I thought he was only a driver and a bodyguard."

Both women raised their brows. "A bodyguard?" Noreen echoed.

"A driver!" Brianna exclaimed. "Tyce owns one of the biggest investigative and security agencies in the country. He's got teams of highly trained detectives and protection agents in several states. I hadn't heard of him ever personally acting as a bodyguard or a driver."

"With someone as famous as Claire, though, he probably made an exception," Noreen conceded. "He obviously wanted to make sure she had the best protection possible."

"But at the time, he didn't know my real identity," Claire argued. Uncomprehending frowns settled over their faces. "My cousin hired him," she explained, "and gave him a false name for me. Tyce thought I was Claire Jones, a prize-winning poet."

Noreen tilted her head. Brianna rested her chin on her fist. Both women stared at her with deepening frowns. A little inkling of unease skittered down Claire's spine. "He *would* personally guard a prizewinning poet...right?"

"Right," they chimed in unison, nodding a little too emphatically.

Claire bit her bottom lip. Whether they believed it or not, he hadn't known she was Valentina Richmond when he'd taken on the assignment. It had come as quite a shock to him.

"Of *course* he'd personally guard a prizewinning poet," Noreen attested, more convincingly this time. "Poets are important, too. Aren't they, Brianna?"

"Oh, yes, very important."

"Anyway," said Noreen with a dismissive wave, "around here, he's considered a hero. And if you have any doubt about Brianna or me keeping the secret that you're here, well...don't. There's not too much we wouldn't do for Tyce Walker."

Claire nodded with a grateful smile.

"I hope you'll get the chance to know him, Claire," Brianna said. "He might not say much or show what he's thinking, but under that granite exterior, he's a compassionate man. You can trust him to do whatever's best for you."

A lump rose in Claire's throat. They thought she didn't know him. Maybe she didn't, but she *felt* that she did. She felt that she knew him better than she'd known anyone in her entire life.

"Let's finish with your checkup," murmured Noreen, adjusting the stethoscope to her ears. "You took a pretty good bump to your head and you've got a few nasty bruises, as I'm sure you've figured out by now." Brushing open the collar of the oversize man's shirt Claire was wearing—a shirt Claire had never seen before—the doctor pressed the stethoscope to her chest and listened. She then took her pulse and asked questions about pain and dizziness. "Stay in bed for the rest of today," she finally pronounced. "By tomorrow you should be up and around. I'll give you a pill for that headache."

"She's awake?"

The hopeful, masculine voice at the bedroom door turned the doctor around and set Claire's pulse to leaping. Tyce. He looked worn and worried and so dear to her that her heart rose into her throat. He didn't look injured; at least, not that she could see from a distance. His gaze locked with hers as he crossed the room. "Claire!"

She sat up, and without giving it a thought, reached for him. He came straight into her arms, catching her to him in a tender embrace. "I was so damn worried about you," he whispered hoarsely.

"Oh, Tyce." She pressed her face against his neck, tears of relief clouding her eyes as she savored his strength, his warmth, his wholeness. "Are you really okay?"

"Me?" He cast a quick glance at the two women who stood gaping, and they immediately turned away into a discussion of their own. Lowering his voice to a husky whisper, he said to Claire, "What about you? You scared the living hell out of me." His breath stirred her hair as he rested his cheek against her temple. "Are you in a lot of pain?"

"No, no. I'm just so glad to see you're okay."

"The explosion knocked you off your feet, and you hit your head." He brushed the hair out of her face and dashed her tears away with his thumbs. "Thank God, you were wearing that crazy wig. It was ugly as hell, but it cushioned you just enough."

"Ugly?" A protesting half smile trembled on her lips. "You didn't like me as a brunette?"

"I like you any way, *every* way..." he whispered devoutly, placing a kiss against her forehead. "Except dead. When I saw you lying there against that tree—" His voice broke off, his muscles clenched.

She pressed her cheek against his and closed her eyes, warmed by the emotion she'd seen in his gaze. "You saved me. You saved my life. Again. First from a demented kid on a Boogie board, then from a booby-trapped pickup truck."

His arms tightened around her, and for a moment he just held her.

She pulled back to read his eyes. "Did you get hurt? You must have." Before he realized it, she'd unbuttoned his shirt halfway down.

"What are you doing?"

"I want to see for myself. I can't believe you're not hurt at all." He caught her hands, but she'd already managed to tug his shirt off one shoulder. "You are! You're cut! I see a gash. Dr. Myers," she called, remembering the other two women who were presumably still present, "did you see this gash?"

"For God's sake, Claire," Tyce protested with an embarrassed laugh, shrugging his shirt back onto his golden, muscled shoulder, "it's nothing."

"It is. It's a deep cut." In her most regal manner, she commanded, "Take off your shirt."

"No, I'm not taking off my shirt."

With an exasperated sigh, she swept her hands down his muscle-corded arms, which were suspiciously concealed by long sleeves. "Are you hurt somewhere else, too?"

"He bandaged his right forearm," confirmed Noreen from the foot of the bed. "Wouldn't even let me do it. And his ankle was so swollen last night he couldn't keep his shoe on."

"Thanks a lot, Doc," he muttered dryly. "She needed to know that."

Claire held his lean, stubble-roughened face between her hands. "I'm so sorry. I nearly got you killed!"

"That's the craziest thing I've ever heard. If either of us is to blame, it should be me. It was my job to protect you. Wait till I get my hands on the bastard who—"

"You're not going after the bomber, are you? Please don't, Tyce. It's too dangerous. Let the police handle it."

"Do you want me to tell the police that you were with me in the truck when it exploded? If I do, it'll hit the worldwide news in minutes flat. The police, maybe even the FBI, will contact you for questioning, and when they do, the bomber will get a chance to find you. As it is, he doesn't know if you're alive or dead. You can stay here, under armed guard, while I handle the investigation *my* way. It's up to you."

Thoroughly miserable at the choice facing her, she wrung her hands and silently debated with herself. She was so afraid of endangering his life again. "I could go home," she said. "I have personal protection agents who guard me."

"I won't let you go anywhere until I know you're safe. First we have to…" He hesitated, as if hating to broach a subject. "We have to figure out who would want to kill you."

A chilly feeling of dread wormed its way through her. "There's a man who has been stalking me and sending hate mail."

"He's definitely a suspect, and I'll be checking up on him. We also have to look at…others. People you know. Someone who…might stand to gain something from your death."

She didn't want to talk about this. Didn't want to even think about it. "You mean my family, don't you?"

"Who would inherit your money in the event of your death?"

Old questions reared up, doubts digging in with new ferocity. For so many years she'd wondered if her relatives loved her. Now she had to wonder if they had attempted to kill her. "If I die without a child of my own," she murmured, "the money would be divided among my family." She focused a pained gaze on him. "I understand there's plenty to go around."

He gathered her to him and cradled her against his chest. "I'm sorry, Claire. I know this must be painful for you. I'll do everything I can to find the bomber. And if he was hired to do it, I'll find out by whom."

"Does that mean you're leaving?"

"I have to."

"Please don't go. If you must, then I'll go with you."

"No way in hell. Promise me you'll stay here."

"Promise me you'll come back."

He tightened his embrace, shutting his eyes and rocking her.

Behind them, the women slanted each other a glance. Brianna cleared her throat and called, "We're, uh, going to go clean up the kitchen, and then, uh, catch up on some sleep. Just call if you need anything."

The embracing couple acknowledged with only the slightest of nods. The interlopers withdrew from the room.

"Something tells me," Noreen said, closing the door behind them, "there's been a lot more going on there than bodyguarding."

will understand now." He murmured, the intonation of those words taking her back to Ranger's cabin, back on him, he studied her closely and ... him, her close. From the photo group, linger ...

9

BY THE TIME he forced himself to leave her, Tyce felt as if an invisible cord had wrapped around his heart, and that if he ventured too far away from her, that cord might cut him in half.

Crazy, to feel so damn desperate.

Crazy to have kissed her. But the moment the bedroom door had closed behind Noreen and Brianna, he'd given in to a kiss he'd craved in a profound, bewildering way.

The kiss gradually turned from tender to needful, and he found himself wanting to disregard both his wounds and hers and make slow, fortifying love to her. She seemed to want that, too, pulling him down with her onto the pillows and kissing him with an urgency that hardened his body and electrified his blood. He wanted to merge with her, fill her so completely that they couldn't ever fully separate again.

As the kiss ebbed and surged, she opened the shirt she wore, and he filled his palms with her breasts. She sobbed and moaned and kissed him deeper.

Neither of them actually undressed. They unbuttoned, unzipped and shoved aside all barriers until skin pressed against skin. Her hands found his hardness. He found her softness. With his jeans pushed down to his thighs, he levered himself into her, deep into her tight, velvet heat.

Locked to her in ultimate closeness, dazed by a bliss that transcended pleasure, he didn't want to move. He wanted to stay as they were, to savor the intensity for as long as humanly possible. But the need to move grew to a throbbing ache as her tightness gripped him in subtle undulations. He caught at her hips to force her into stillness, but it did no good. He himself couldn't stop now, any more than the sea could stop its tides. The pleasure, the need, the sweet sharp emotion escalated to a feverish pitch.

As he strained to hold his climax at bay, she rasped against his ear, "I love you, Tyce. I love you!"

Neither heaven nor hell could stop him then. He thrust into her with such a forceful need to possess that they both cried out, detonating the explosion. The repercussions shocked him, rocked him, body and soul. And as he clutched her to him in trembling awe, he grappled with a dawning truth. He wanted her words to be true. He wanted her to love him...*because he loved her.* Deeply, mindlessly, with no possible good end in sight.

He loved her. Her laughter, her humor, her smile. Her beauty and her naiveté. Her warmth. Her body. He loved making love to her, and didn't want to stop. Ever.

Of all the idiotic, self-destructive needs known

to man, this senseless desire for her had to be one of the worst. Even if she'd meant the words that she'd whispered, she was saying them to the man she *thought* he was—the man who had eased her loneliness and protected her from danger with no ulterior motives clouding the issue. She knew nothing of the real Tyce Walker, the man hired to betray her. The man who'd disregarded all the damning secrets he kept and made love to her. She would despise that man.

Slowly he eased his arms out from around her, tormented by his guilt. Loving her only made the guilt worse.

She glanced up at him, and her tender smile faltered. "Tyce? Are you hurting?"

"No." He was, but not in the way she meant. He wished he could tell her how and why, but if he did, she would probably leave. He couldn't chance that. The bomber was out there somewhere, hunting for her. The danger was simply too grave to risk telling her now.

"Tyce," she said again, her face warm with an alluring shyness, "if what I said made you uncomfortable, please, forget it. The words just slipped out somehow."

He tried to contrive a smile, but didn't quite succeed. So she hadn't meant them. He should be glad. "I suppose we've all said crazy things at one time or another, in the heat of the moment."

Her golden brows drew together, and a little frown darkened her eyes. "It might be crazy, and I hadn't intended to tell you, but I...I meant what

I said. I've never felt this way about anyone before."

An odd mix of emotion kicked him in the chest—gladness that she'd meant it, incredulity that she could, and regret so strong it nearly choked him. If only things were different. If only she wasn't a billionaire celebrity, and he hadn't been hired to tail her. But wishes like those only made the reality harder to face.

"Don't trust feelings like that right now, Claire," he warned. "Danger has a way of twisting emotions around, making them into something they're not. You've been alone, and lonely, and vulnerable. And I...well, I was lucky enough to be there for you." His voice dropped to a husky murmur. "And we've been intimate." He couldn't help touching her silken hair, smoothing a lock of it from her face. "I'm no psychologist, but I can understand how all that might lead us to feel...something for each other."

"So you do feel...something...for me?"

Their gazes heated, and against his will, a whisper tore from deep inside of him. "Yes. I feel something for you."

The admission wrapped around them like a sheltering, intimate cocoon, blocking out everything except the two of them. A profound happiness illuminated her eyes, making him love her with a fierceness that scared him.

"You don't have to say anything more." Her smile was softer than a caress. "That's all I need to know."

"No, damn it, Claire, it isn't!" The harshness of the rebuke brought a startled flush to her cheeks. He shut his eyes and compressed his lips, trying to rein in his self-directed anger. When he again met her gaze, he managed to gentle his voice. "You don't know me, Princess. There are things about me that you wouldn't like."

"What things?"

Staring into her incredibly beautiful, trusting eyes, he knew that nothing in his life would hurt him more than having to tell her. Blowing out a rush of breath that had caught in his throat, he forced himself up from the bed. "I don't have time to go into it right now. I've got a flight to catch."

The pain that shot up his leg as he stood and zipped up his jeans reminded him of their injuries, both his and hers. He turned to her in concern, hating himself for forgetting her physical condition. "Claire, are you okay? Did I hurt you?"

"Physically, you mean?" She gave him a wry smile. "No. I'm just a little dizzy." As he shrugged out of his shirt to change into a fresh one, she noticed his injured forearm. A crimson stain was spreading across the bandage. "You're bleeding!"

"I'll take care of it."

"Have Noreen look at it."

"I'm already running late." He changed his shirt and strode toward the door, intending to shower in the guest bathroom and leave without another goodbye. Too much emotion clogged his throat as it was.

"Tyce," she called. Reluctantly he stopped near the door and glanced back at her. She bit down on the corner of her full bottom lip, her gaze excruciatingly tender. "Don't get yourself killed."

Unable to reply, he nodded and left her, feeling as if his heart were tearing in half. He would find the bomber and any co-conspirators and put them behind bars. And then he would tell her everything, the entire truth about his reason for finding her. He owed her at least that much.

But he harbored no false hope. She would despise him for his duplicity. And even if by some miracle she didn't, there could be no future for them. She was American royalty, a beautiful bright star who would soon return to her celestial orbit.

And he, regardless of how much money he had or would make, would always be a kid from the streets.

CLAIRE SPENT the next few days worrying about Tyce's safety and her own, jumping at every unexpected sound or shadow, and holding her breath whenever the phone rang. What would she do if Tyce was killed? Even though she'd known him only a short while, she felt a soul-deep connection with him, one that ruled her entire heart, mind and body. She missed him with an unbearable ache, and longed to hear his voice, see his face, feel his touch.

She was in love with him.

What, she wondered, was the "something" he'd admitted feeling for her?

Sexual desire, certainly. There was no mistaking the heat that pulsed between them whenever they were together, or the passion whenever they made love. But she believed he felt more than that. She believed he was falling in love with her. That belief filled her with such a sweet, giddy joy that even these worrisome days without him seemed magical.

To distract herself from the highs of feeling loved and the lows of fearing for his safety, she took full advantage of the company offered by Brianna and Noreen. They dropped in for frequent visits, the only visitors allowed by the guards who patrolled the property. Brianna brought shorts, tops, sandals and other clothing that she'd bought for Claire at a local department store. Noreen kept a close watch on her physical condition.

Tyce called every day. He reported little progress in his investigation, and never stayed on the phone long, but she looked forward to his calls with a ridiculous yearning. "If all goes well, I'll be back by Sunday," he'd promised during his last phone call.

Sunday. She hoped he could keep that promise. She began counting the hours.

On Friday, both Brianna and Noreen spent the night. A "pajama party," they'd laughingly called it. They listened to music, drank wine and taught

Claire how to play rummy. She taught them how to curtsy to a queen. As the hour grew late and they lounged on pillows strewn across the living room, their conversations grew personal.

Claire couldn't help mentioning Tyce and the funny, touching things he'd said or done.

"You seem to care about him," Brianna noted.

"I do," she whispered, her love for him welling up inside of her until she felt sure it must glow from her eyes.

"He seems to care about you, too," remarked Noreen. "I've never seen him act or talk the way he did with you. I thought about checking him for fever!"

"Women in town have been chasing him for years," Brianna put in. "He hasn't let anyone, male or female, get close enough to know him well. He holds us all at a distance."

Bothered by this insight, Claire chewed her lip for a moment. "He holds me at a distance, too," she confided. "Maybe not a physical one, but…"

They pondered the enigma of Tyce Walker in silence.

"I think it has to do with Joe," Noreen finally pronounced.

"Joe?" repeated Claire. "Who's Joe?"

"I don't know the whole story, but I gathered some of it from his letters. You see, Brianna and I have been helping Tyce in his effort to get justice for his kids. You know, street kids who were thrown into jail unjustly. We keep in touch with them through letters while Tyce gathers evidence on their behalf. There's only one prisoner writing to us who's an adult. Joe."

"But what can he have to do with Tyce personally?"

"They were kids together in a foster home." Noreen's voice grew solemn. "Things got bad, and they ran away. Lived on the streets of L.A. One night, some thugs jumped them with pipes and chains. One of the thugs died, and Joe...well, he was sent to prison as an adult. The cops called it murder."

"Murder!" exclaimed Claire. "It sounds more like self-defense."

"He was given life without parole."

Claire grew heartsick just thinking about it. It could have been Tyce, she realized.

"Tyce gets real intense whenever Joe's name is mentioned," Noreen said softly. "I think he blames himself. The thugs were after Tyce for some reason. Joe just happened to be there."

"Do you have any letters from Joe and the other kids?" Claire asked.

"Sure. I have a stack of them in my car that I brought to divvy up with Brianna."

"Could I help read and answer them?"

"I don't see why not. We can use the help."

Claire retired to Tyce's bed with a stack of letters. One was from Joe. His handwriting was nearly illegible, his spelling atrocious and the letter started off with, "Yo! How goes it, ladies?" He talked about trivialities—oatmeal cookies that someone named "Hattie" had sent him, a television cop show he liked, and a fight going on in the next cell. His humor made Claire smile, and though he didn't actually thank anybody for anything, his appreciation that someone cared came through so loud and clear that her throat tightened. He finished with, "Remind Tyce that my team beat his last Sunday. Ha, ha."

She wanted very much to help Joe. And for some reason, she loved Tyce all the more.

As she set the letter aside, she felt vaguely ashamed of her childhood belief that poor children led happier lives than she. Her wealth had kept her isolated, but it had also kept her safe.

She also realized that she was still under guard, still virtually imprisoned, but now had no desire to run away. She felt needed, and strong, and hopeful that she could find a way to tear down the walls Tyce had built around his heart.

Early the next morning, while her two guests were still sleeping, a guard from somewhere on the property called on a walkie-talkie. "Sorry to disturb you, Ms. Jones, but a lady by the name of Hattie Pitts brought a package for Mr. Walker. She says it's urgent that he gets it immediately."

"Hattie? Did you say Hattie?" Claire remembered the name from Joe's letter. Could it be the same woman?

"Yes, ma'am. I have orders from Mr. Walker to keep everyone out, so I sent her on her way. But she left this package. I opened it to be sure there were no electronic devices in it. It looks like a letter and photographs. I'd forward it to Mr. Walker, but he told me this morning that he'll be back to-night."

"Tonight?" Anticipation lightened her heart. "Just bring the package to the house, then. I'll be sure he gets it."

Within moments, a square-faced, burly man in a security uniform met her at the door. With a sunny smile for him and for the beautiful, fresh-scented summer morning, she took the package, thanked him and relocked the door.

The preprinted return address read The Global Gazette.

She stiffened. She knew that name. It was a tab-loid...*the* tabloid that had published the photos of Preston and her bridesmaids. Why would this woman named Hattie be sending an urgent pack-age to Tyce from the *Global Gazette*?

She pulled out the letter and the photos. In dry-mouthed dismay, she flipped through them. They were pictures of her—on the beach, near the pool, in the condominium lobby. Then came pictures that included Tyce—the two of them walking on the beach, riding on a Jet Ski, dancing at the beach bar and talking near the sand dunes.

She hadn't realized how *intimate* they'd looked.

The last photo wrenched a cry from her. It was a close-up of their passionate kiss in the corridor of their condo.

The violation of her privacy sickened her. What did she have to do, where did she have to hide, to escape this torment? And now she'd brought Tyce into the public spotlight. His past and present would be mercilessly examined, and his business would surely suffer. Would he come to hate her for it?

With her heart in her throat, she unfolded and read the letter that accompanied the photos.

T.K.—

I can delay the publication of these photos for only a day or so. Hope you know how much this delay will cost me. I have the jump on the competition, but for how long? Anyway, I've included the crowd shots you've requested.

I also wanted to remind you about the photos that might still be in the microcamera of your sunglasses. *If* you took any more, that is.

Enclosed is a partial payment of your fee. Send me your receipts for expenses incurred so far and I'll reimburse you.

—Hattie

P.S. What do you think of the headline
The Princess & The P.I.?

Claire stared at the letter and its attachment in numb disbelief. This couldn't be what it seemed. Tyce couldn't possibly be "T.K."

Her hands trembled as she found the check stapled to the letter. It was from the *Global Gazette*. Made out to Tyce Walker. For "Investigative Services, V. Richmond."

10

SHE'LL BE HAPPY, Tyce thought as he drove a rented car to the Los Angeles airport. He knew how upset Claire had been to think that the bomber could be someone in her family.

He would set her mind at ease when he got home. The stalker had been the one who planted the bomb, after all. Tyce's team of investigators had dredged up clues that led back to Los Angeles.

Evidence pointed to Malcolm Forte, the thirty-year-old son of her uncle's secretary. He hadn't known Claire personally, but seemed to fixate on her when his mother began working for Edgar Richmond last year. Through his mother, Malcolm had gotten access to the report Tyce had submitted. He then concentrated his efforts on finding Tyce's agents who were working on the case. A clever sociopath. The most dangerous kind.

The challenge now was to find enough hard proof to put him away. They'd matched his movements to the stalker's previous intrusions and the vandalism to Claire's New York town house. They'd searched his apartment where they'd found weapons and explosives. Malcolm's alibi for the day of the bombing was weak, but Tyce still needed evidence that placed him in Panama City Beach.

He'd thought of the photographs he and presumably Hattie had taken of Claire. What if they'd inadvertently captured Malcolm's face in one of those photos?

Hattie hadn't yet returned his calls. She'd been out of the office, he was told. Knowing her, she was still hunting for Claire. At least she hadn't yet published any of the photos he was sure she'd taken…maybe because of the dire threats he'd left along with his request for the photos.

He dialed his office number on his cell phone and asked his secretary if any packages had arrived from Hattie Pitts.

"No, sir, but yesterday she was nosing around the airport where we keep the corporate jet. She introduced herself to the pilot as your mother. He swears he didn't tell her much, but can't remember exactly what he *did* say."

Tyce's muscles tightened with foreboding. After the explosion, he'd flown Claire to Ohio. His pilot could have easily mentioned the recent trip. Hattie knew Tyce owned a cabin in Ohio. It wouldn't take her long to pinpoint his property…and to find Claire.

Cursing beneath his breath, he disconnected from his secretary and prepared to call his guards at the cabin. As he began to dial, the phone rang.

Brad Demming, the guard he'd left in charge, blurted, "Ms. Jones just left with Dr. Myers. I tried to stop them, but Ms. Jones said she'd sue me for false imprisonment.''

''False imprisonment!''

''She's madder than hell, sir. I think it might have something to do with the package I gave her from Hattie Pitts.''

Tyce cursed out loud this time—cursed Hattie for her meddling, the guard for his naiveté, and himself for hurting Claire.

I love you, Tyce, she'd told him.

He felt as if a punishing fist had grabbed hold of his heart. How betrayed she must be feeling! He had to talk to her.

''Follow her, Brad. Keep her under guard. And stay in contact with me.''

''Yes, sir.''

Swerving over onto the shoulder of the Los Angeles freeway, Tyce stopped the car, shut his eyes and struggled to marshal his thoughts. She'd seen the photos he'd requested from Hattie. God only knew what kind of pictures Hattie had added to the ones he'd taken, or what kind of note she'd included.

Fumbling for his wallet, he found the number of Noreen's cell phone. It rang a few times before she answered.

''Noreen, do you have Claire with you?''

''Tyce! Am I glad to hear from you. I don't know what's going on, friend, but you owe Claire one heck of an explanation.''

''Let me talk to her.''

''Great idea.'' But after a moment, Noreen came

back on the line, sounding subdued. "She doesn't want to talk. And as much as I hate to get in the middle of this, I notice that one of your guards is following us. Is Claire still in danger, or, uh, does he intend to take pictures of her?"

Tyce gritted his teeth. He deserved that. "I don't pay my guards to take pictures. She needs to be protected. Let Brad accompany her. Where are you taking her?"

"I'm sorry, Tyce, but she doesn't want me to say."

With a frustrated sigh, he leaned his head back against the seat. "Tell her we've found the bomber. We have him under constant surveillance, and we're looking for enough evidence to have him arrested. Turns out he's Malcolm Forte, the son of her uncle's secretary."

He heard Noreen repeat what he'd told her, and a soft exclamation in reply. His hand tightened around the phone. "*Please*, Noreen, just give the phone to Claire."

"Okay, but I can't guarantee she'll talk."

A few moments of silence went by, and he heard Noreen urging her to at least listen. Noreen stopped talking, and Tyce formed a mental image of Claire sitting there with her lips compressed, holding the phone reluctantly to her ear.

"Claire, are you there?" He received no reply, but went on anyway. "Claire, I'm sorry! I never meant to hurt you. I never meant to…oh, hell. I didn't know you when I took Hattie's case. I didn't know…" *I didn't know I'd fall in love with you.* But he couldn't say that now. He'd sound like the worst kind of opportunist, a con man trying to play back into her good graces. "I was going to tell you the truth, I swear, but I couldn't until I found the bomber. I knew you'd leave the minute I'd confessed. It was too dangerous to risk having you run off, like you're doing now." After another moment of tense silence, he said in a rough whisper, "Just let me know if you're listening."

An inarticulate sound came through to him, and after a moment, she whispered, "Johnny hadn't sent you. And you knew who I was from the very start."

He closed his eyes and gripped the phone harder. "Yes."

"You knew I wasn't a poet."

If it hadn't hurt so much, that statement might have made him smile. "Yes."

She was silent for so long that he knew she was remembering all the times and ways he had lied to her. "I was such a fool," she whispered.

"I never thought that, Claire."

"Did you take pictures of me for a tabloid?"

"Only a few. Beach shots. Ones that anyone could have taken."

"I'd say it's apparent that your cohorts had to have taken the others—the ones that show you and me...together..." Her voice, sounding choked, faded into silence.

"Claire, you can't believe that I'd knowingly allow someone to take pictures of...of *us!*"

"You weren't there to be my bodyguard at all...were you?"

"Not officially. But—"

"How did you know my assumed name and my travel plans?"

He opened his mouth, but no words came out. He couldn't tell her that Hattie had bugged her cousin's phone, or Hattie could be arrested. It might serve her right—in fact, he might glean some definite pleasure from it—but he couldn't betray the woman who had once saved him from himself. "I'm sorry, Claire, but I can't—"

Their connection went dead.

With it went his glimmer of hope that he'd somehow find a way to see her, to touch her, to hold her, at least one more time. He wouldn't, he realized. Ever again.

THE SMALL JET that she had asked Johnny to charter for her was ready by the time she and Noreen reached the private airport. She would have chartered the jet herself except she hadn't wanted to use her own name on the charge account. She knew better. The media would have been there to greet her in droves. She wouldn't be surprised if they were, anyhow. Tyce Walker's guard was still tailing her, which could mean trouble.

She was going home.

So much for finding freedom outside her sheltered world. There was no such thing for her. She'd have to make her own kind of freedom—by assuming absolute control.

"I hate to see you leave like this," said Noreen, her dark eyes troubled as she handed Claire the small overnight bag of clothing that Brianna had bought for her earlier that week. "Maybe you should give Tyce a chance to explain."

Claire adjusted the large sunglasses Brianna had also bought for her. She needed them not to guard against sun on this overcast morning, but to help preserve her identity during the flight. She tried not to remember how her previous efforts to do that very thing had been so deviously foiled. She tried not to think about the silver sunglasses Tyce had used on the beach to take pictures of her. He'd had a microcamera built in their frame. "He's explained all I need to know."

"I don't blame you for being angry and hurt, but I still think he cares about you. A lot."

Claire swung the strap of the overnight bag over her shoulder and felt a light drizzle against her face. It reminded her of the sea mist as she'd ridden on a Jet Ski through rainbows. A knot tightened in her chest. "He's a convincing actor. I'd say he missed his calling, but—" she forced a small, grim smile "—he seems to be very good at what he does."

"Claire!" Noreen caught her shoulders and held her in a firm grip, her gaze forcing its way past the coldness that had descended to shield her from the worst of the pain. "Don't close in on yourself. You have so much warmth and good-ness to share."

"I have money. And houses, and yachts, and

lots of...things. That's what I'll share...when I feel like it." Claire glanced away to fight the tightening in her throat. "I'd like to still help out with the letters to the prisoners. Now that I know about those kids, I can't turn my back on them."

"I'll arrange for some of the letters to be sent to you."

Claire gave her a quick, hard hug. "Thank you for everything. I'll never forget the time I spent with you." Before her control could slip, she hurried to the jet.

The flight was long and tedious, but gave her time to think. She'd do all she could to help the kids she'd learned about from Noreen and Brianna. Large sums of money might help grease the wheels of justice.

She also decided to have her uncle move out of her home, to replace any employees she didn't want to keep, and to meet with her bankers to inspect her investment portfolio.

The time had come to take charge of her affairs.

Once she had, she would finance some eager inventor to come up with gadgets to foil the paparazzi's cameras. Ultraviolet rays that would flash from her hat, maybe. Lasers that her bodyguards could shoot to damage film. Who knew what could be invented? She'd make it well worth the inventor's time.

And she'd keep a bevy of private investigators on her payroll to monitor the media's movements regarding her. Let the paparazzi—the most annoying ones—feel the frustration of having to deal with a constant tail. She'd also buy stock in as many tabloids as she could, affect their management decisions from within. They'd declared war, and she meant to fight it.

When the jet finally landed in Los Angeles, her protection agents and chauffeur met her. She rode home in utter silence.

Her first order to her staff when she walked in the door of her Beverly Hills home was, "I'll take no calls and see no visitors. *None.*"

THE POLICE ARRESTED the son of her uncle's secretary three days after Claire had returned home. Malcolm Forte was charged with a number of crimes ranging from stalking to attempted murder. His mother resigned from her post, and Uncle Edgar was now in the process of hiring a new secretary.

Uncle Edgar was also preparing his beach house to become his residence. He'd been shocked and indignant when Claire asked him to move, but she'd refused to relent. He had plenty money of his own now, which she'd guessed long ago. It seemed to be killing him, though, to realize that his influence over her—or rather, over her fortune—no longer carried much weight. He still hoped for a reconciliation between her and Preston, which would cement his tie with the family. He'd always been involved with California politics and hated to see a solid alliance foiled.

She'd only rolled her eyes at the suggestion. Preston and his infidelity no longer hurt her.

He belonged to another world.

She'd grown up since then.

Throughout the entire week following Malcolm's arrest, she saw her name and face in the news as the stalker's intended victim. From her attorney, whom she instructed to follow the case, she learned that Malcolm had been caught in a photograph of her taken in Florida, which disproved his alibi.

At least she now understood why Tyce had requested those photos from Hattie. His hunch had apparently paid off. But that didn't exonerate him for taking them in the first place. The very idea hurt more than any other betrayal ever had.

Bracing herself for the worst, Claire sent a courier out to fetch her the latest tabloids. She told herself she didn't care what appeared in the *Global Gazette*, but she held her breath as she waited. When the courier returned with the tabloids, she hurried down the long, shadowy corridors to her bedroom, where she locked the door and spread the papers out on her bed. With nimble fingers, she flipped through their pages, looking for the photos she'd been dreading to see.

Oddly enough, all she found were stories that focused on the stalking, with relatively old photographs of her.

Why?

She knew only too well that the *Global Gazette* had plenty of sensational photographs to choose from. In many that she remembered, she'd looked like a reckless, wanton creature who'd fallen hopelessly in love.

It was the truth. She'd fallen in love with Tyce Walker, and had believed he was falling in love with her.

Why hadn't those photos been published?

The next morning she searched the daily newspapers for photos and came across a small one of Tyce that acknowledged his part in solving the case. Although Claire was mentioned as Malcolm's intended victim, not a word connected her to Tyce.

She found herself cutting his photo out of the newspaper. It made no sense, this compelling desire to keep his memory close to her heart. He'd hurt her, humiliated her and betrayed her.

He'd also made her feel more alive than she ever had. He'd given her a taste, even if it were a false one, of being loved. How would she ever manage to forget him? Certainly not by keeping a picture of him that she'd cut out of the newspaper!

As she tried to talk herself into throwing the picture away, her uncle strode onto the sunny veranda where she lingered over her morning coffee.

"The moving van will be coming soon for my furniture. I—" He stopped beside her breakfast table, his attention caught by the picture. "That's that Tyce Walker, isn't it? What are you doing with a picture of him?"

"It was in today's newspaper," she mumbled,

embarrassed to be caught with it. When her uncle's disapproval registered, she drew her brows together in puzzlement. "Do you know him?"

"Of course. He's done investigative work for me for years."

She stared at him in surprise. She couldn't have heard him right. "Tyce Walker worked for you?"

"I employed his services to gather information on various candidates. Walker usually does a damn fine job. That's why I hired him to find you."

Claire's head spun with incredulity. "*You* hired him?"

"The way you called off your wedding and took off on your own, I felt sure you were involved with bad company. I hired Walker to find you and keep you under surveillance."

While Claire struggled to absorb this information, Edgar sat beside her with an angry scowl. "Walker found you, all right...then after one lousy report, he refused to let me know where you were. I was worried sick, Valentina. Sick!"

Claire stared at him in confusion. How could Tyce have been hired by both Hattie Pitts and Uncle Edgar?

With a scoffing laugh, he went on. "I think Walker suspected I had something to do with that bombing. Can you imagine? The upstart! I gave him an ultimatum—to either turn over a full report on you, or forget the favor he'd asked." Vengefully, he muttered, "He can kiss that favor goodbye."

Claire's heart turned over. "What favor?"

"Some friend of his, in jail for murder. Walker wanted me to pull strings to get him a new trial. Ha! He made his choice when he refused to say where you were. Like I told him then and I'd tell him now—that fellow will rot in jail before I'll lift a finger to help him."

Questions and emotions flooded Claire. "Was his friend's name Joe?"

"Yes, I believe it was. How did you know?"

But Claire's mind was no longer engaged in the conversation.

Tyce had refused to betray her! Even knowing it would cost him the chance to free Joe, he'd refused to tell her uncle where she was. Grappling with the enormity of that discovery, she sank back into the wrought-iron patio chair as her uncle muttered something and left her.

Why had Tyce done it? He'd stood to gain everything by submitting the report to her uncle and to lose too much by withholding it. He really had been protecting her, she realized in a daze, although no one had hired him to do so. He'd chosen her safety over Joe's freedom.

How did his assignment from Hattie fit into the picture?

And why hadn't those photos been published?

I never meant to hurt you, he'd said. *I didn't know you then.*

She'd been so sure of him, back at his cabin. She'd trusted him implicitly. Could she have been that wrong?

Her head pounded with troubling questions; her heart spun with hopes, doubts and fears. But one truth gradually emerged as all important: she had to trust in her own judgment.

She would do whatever it took to find the answers to her questions.

Before she set out to do so, however, she summoned her uncle for another brief chat. "Uncle Edgar, am I to understand that you hired Tyce Walker to follow me because you were worried about my safety?"

Though he flushed a subtle shade of red, he swore that her safety had been first and foremost in his mind.

"Then I'd say Tyce Walker has done an excellent job, wouldn't you?"

Nonplussed, he pursed his lips and looked as if he'd like to argue. He couldn't, of course.

"Pull whatever strings are necessary to get justice for his friend Joe," Claire instructed. "New evidence has been found that must be considered."

"But—"

"If there's a problem, I'll look into the matter myself. I intend to support the politicians of my choice financially, anyway. Might as well learn the characters of the ones in office now, right?"

He assured her he'd have someone look into Joe's case immediately.

"Oh, and Uncle Edgar... Don't ever have me followed again."

CURIOUS FACES PEERED out of office windows as the stretch limousine pulled into the parking lot beside the old brick building that housed the *Global Gazette.* Ensconced behind the heavily tinted windows in the very back of the limo, Claire gave instructions to her driver.

She had no intention of walking into the lion's den, or allowing Hattie Pitts too much time to prepare for her visit.

Per her instructions, her driver dialed a cell phone and informed the party at the other end that he was calling from the parking lot. His employer wished to see Ms. Hattie Pitts—alone. *Now.* He then hung up.

It didn't take long for a barrel-chested young man wearing a security uniform and carrying a handheld radio to emerge from the building, approach the limo and tap on the driver's window.

The driver lowered the window, but only to his eye level.

"You the ones here to see Hattie Pitts?" the security officer asked.

"Yes," the chauffeur replied. "Tell her we won't wait long."

With a glance toward the back of the limo—a glance that could reveal nothing about the occupant behind the tinted windows—he asked, "Who should I say is here?"

The chauffeur, a middle-aged man with Old World arrogance, replied coolly, "You may say whomever you'd like."

The young guard flushed, muttered something

into his handheld radio, then replied, "Can't see her unless you give a name."

"Very well." The driver raised his window and started up the engine.

The limo hadn't moved but a couple yards when the security officer thumped on the fender, yelling, "Hey! Wait a minute." With the engine idling, the chauffeur lowered the window again and merely gazed at the irate guard. Grudgingly, the guard muttered, "She says she'll be right down. But there better not be any funny business. I've got your plate number, pal."

Claire had suspected that Hattie Pitts's curiosity might overrule other considerations.

Within moments, a petite older woman emerged from the building and walked with a no-nonsense briskness toward the limo, her eyes shaded by heavy black sunglasses, a cigarette protruding from the side of her mouth. Her short black-and-gray hair stuck up in disorderly tufts, and her brown pantsuit looked as if she'd slept in it. She didn't waste time approaching the driver, but went directly to the back and rapped on the window.

With a touch of a button, Claire lowered the tinted glass, bringing the woman's gracelessly aging face into clear view—at least, what she could see of it around the sunglasses. "Are you Hattie Pitts?"

The woman blatantly gaped openmouthed at Claire, her cigarette precariously hanging on her bottom lip. "Well, if this don't beat all." Biting down on the cigarette, she said in a gravelly voice, "Yeah, I'm Hattie. What d'ya want?"

"If you're interested in knowing," Claire replied in her most autocratic tone, "get in, Ms. Pitts."

Hattie promptly waved her glowering security guard away, opened the door and slid in. Claire raised the tinted window and gave her driver a nod. The limo pulled smoothly out of the parking lot and into the gridlocked streets of Los Angeles. At another touch of a button, a Plexiglas partition hummed into place to separate Claire and her guest from the driver.

"To what do I owe the honor, Princess?"

Holding out her hand, Claire demanded, "Give me your glasses, please."

Hattie's graying brows shot up above the heavy black frames. "You want my glasses?"

"Immediately."

With the hint of a grudging smile, Hattie whisked off her glasses and plunked them into Claire's waiting palm.

Just as she'd suspected, they felt a little too heavy. No doubt they'd been loaded with a film cartridge. Slipping them into her purse, Claire murmured, "You *are* a cagey one, aren't you?"

"I'll take that as a compliment." Hattie assessed her with keen, dark, squinty eyes. The squint, Claire deduced, was probably caused by the smoke from her cigarette. She'd taken a long, hard draw and now exhaled an acrid haze.

"Don't happen to have a stocked bar in this limo, do you?" she asked. "Wouldn't mind a stiff one right about now."

"Sorry, no bar." As the limousine inched its way through downtown traffic, Claire added, "And please...lose the cigarette."

Her passenger scowled as she stubbed out the cigarette in the ashtray. "You have more in common with T.K. than I thought."

The mention of "T.K." caused an extra-hard thumping in Claire's heart. Hattie had addressed Tyce as "T.K." in her note. The very thought of him infused Claire with an astounding ache. "Why haven't those photos of me been published?"

"Hmm. Celebrities usually ask why I *did* publish photos, not why I *didn't*." She lounged back against the seat as leisurely as a queen holding court, yet studied Claire with intense interest. "T.K.'s got 'em."

"Tyce has them? *All* of them?"

"Every last one. Even the negatives."

"Why?"

"He took 'em, that's why. Broke into my office and stole everything I had on you. Should have known he'd do something like that," she grumbled. "Forgot how good he was at breaking and entering."

Claire bit back a sharp retort about honor among thieves. As far as she was concerned, the tabloid had stolen her privacy to take the pictures in the first place. Turnabout's fair play. She was glad Tyce had stolen them. At least, she *thought* she was. Then again... "What's he going to do with them?"

"Knowing T.K., nothing worthwhile. I had to blackmail him into taking them in the first place."

"Blackmail!"

"So to speak. I knew he had inside contacts with your uncle, and figured he might have access to information I couldn't get. Even if he didn't have inside info, I knew he'd find you quicker than anybody. So I bribed him with the only clues I *did* have about your disappearance...and threatened to give them to one of my reporters if he didn't take my case." Hattie shrugged. "A management technique worth learning, Princess. Bribery with a hint of blackmail."

The woman might be unscrupulous, thought Claire, but at least she admitted it. "How did you know which flight I was taking and what my assumed name was going to be?"

"Secrets of the trade."

Vexed, Claire narrowed her eyes. "Did someone in my household spy for you?"

"I wasn't that lucky. Had to go high-tech."

"High-tech? Some kind of electronic surveillance?"

"You don't really think I'd admit to that, do you?"

Thoroughly incensed that she'd been spied upon, Claire sucked in an angry breath, her nostrils flaring. Her voice shook slightly as she inquired, "Did Tyce help you with that, too?"

"Hell, no. Don't ask me why, but he's real touchy when it comes to you. Always has been. He broke a photographer's telescopic lens to keep him from taking candid shots of you through a hotel window." Hattie shook her head disparagingly. "I couldn't imagine what had gotten into that boy."

"When was that?" she asked, highly curious. She hadn't known he'd even seen her, at least in person, before they'd met.

"The night before your debutante ball."

"My debutante ball! That was years ago."

"Seven, to be exact. He quit my tabloid that night, and ratted on his fellow journalists, too. Told your uncle about every stakeout position he knew. That's how he first got hooked up with your uncle."

Revitalizing hope pumped through Claire, and she had to remind herself that not everything Hattie Pitts told her could be trusted. But the need to dig into Tyce's motivations drove her like a compulsion. "You hired Tyce to find me, follow me and take pictures, right?"

Hattie nodded.

"Then why did he pose as my bodyguard? He could have simply tailed me like any other private investigator would have."

A ponderous look came over Hattie's weathered face. "Now there's a good question. Not that it wasn't a splendid ploy. If he had worked it right, we could have gotten some great shots."

Claire stiffened.

Hattie's eyes twinkled unapologetically. "The point is, he didn't. Not one inside photo out of the whole bunch. The only really good ones we got were taken by Sam. And we had to steal the cartridge out of T.K.'s glasses just to get the ones he did take." Looking somewhat disgusted, she grumbled, "When I saw the two of you on that dance floor, I knew he wouldn't be giving me them photos."

A blush warmed Claire's cheeks. "How could you know that?"

Hattie merely uttered a gruff "Ha," as if she had asked a stupid question.

Claire gripped the armrest and looked away, fighting an urge to shake the woman.

"Let's go back to your earlier question." Hattie's face didn't come anywhere near softening, but it somehow lost its harder edges. "There's only one reason I can think of that T.K. posed as your bodyguard. Well, two, actually. The most obvious is to guard you. He's always been the protective sort, and you were definitely in need of protecting. The second reason...well..." She paused, and one end of her mouth kicked up. "I think he made the most of a good opportunity."

Perplexed, Claire held out her hands. "To do what?"

"To be close to you."

Claire stared at her as hope rushed to her head.

Was she crazy to think that this hard-nosed tabloid reporter could possibly have true insight into Tyce's feelings? Afraid of the hope that had kindled in her, she remarked hesitantly, "You seem to know Tyce pretty well."

"As well as anyone does, I guess. I took him in from the streets when he was sixteen. He'd been headed for serious trouble. It was either me or juvenile detention. He chose me."

Curious, Claire couldn't help but ask, "You call him T.K. What's his middle name?"

"Don't know that he has one."

"Then why—"

"My grandfather's name was Theodore Keene, but everyone called him T.K." Hattie's voice softened, almost beyond recognition. "Thought I'd pass down the family name."

Claire's gaze dropped to her hands in her lap. Hattie's relationship to Tyce had become quite clear. She was the closest he had to a mother.

Hattie pulled a pack of cigarettes out of her rumpled suit jacket and tapped one from the pack. "I think I know the question you really want answered, Princess, and it doesn't have anything to do with me." She stuck a cigarette into her mouth and squinted at Claire. "It has to do with T.K. and how he feels about you. Problem is, plain talk won't prove a damn thing to you." Flicking a lighter into flame, she tilted her face, lit her cigarette and inhaled deeply. "Looks like we're going to have to go high-tech."

11

THE CALL, which Tyce had received a week ago, had come as a complete shock. Joe's case would be reexamined. Edgar Richmond had lived up to his promise after all. Tyce couldn't imagine why. Edgar had told him in no uncertain terms that hell would freeze over before he'd help Joe

Something had changed his mind.

Tyce had immediately hired a high-priced attorney to present the evidence he'd found on Joe's behalf. The second shock came at the speed in which the wheels of justice finally turned. By the end of the week, a judge had overturned the conviction.

Joe would be released from prison next Tuesday.

The gut-wrenching relief that the announcement brought Tyce was inherently bittersweet. Joe would finally have his freedom—thank God!—but he'd wasted fourteen years of his life in a prison cell.

The highs and lows left Tyce feeling more or less drained.

He'd decided to take Joe to his cabin in Ohio and let him ease into society at a slower pace than he'd find in Los Angeles. Which meant, of course, that they'd be leaving Los Angeles in a few days' time.

Why, wondered Tyce, should that bother him? This little rented house near his L.A. office never had appealed to him much, especially in the stifling heat of early July, when the smog hung low over the crowded urban streets. Yet, he hated to leave.

Settling down on the sofa wearing only an old pair of cutoffs, he set an icy cola on the table beside him and tried to concentrate on the televised ball game instead of his reason for wanting to stay.

It made no sense.

Just because *she* lived in L.A. didn't mean he'd bump into her on a street corner or at a local grocery store. He had a better chance of finding a designer suit in a Value Village. Even if he camped out on her lawn, chances were he wouldn't see her. According to his inside sources, Claire barely left her private suite within her Beverly Hills mansion, let alone stepped foot outside it. Yet he had this compulsion to stay close at hand.

She doesn't need you anymore. She doesn't want you.

But, God help him, he wanted her. He couldn't sleep, couldn't eat, for wanting her. Everywhere he looked, he saw her face, her eyes, her smile. Every time he closed his eyes, the memory of her kiss branded him again with its heat.

She probably despised him now. When she'd needed someone to trust, he had double-crossed her. When she'd run away to find privacy, he had invaded it. If that weren't bad enough, he'd made love to her under a false pretext. She had no reason on earth to forgive him.

He would certainly never forgive himself. He'd hurt her more deeply than the stalker had. He knew this because he knew the way she loved—with her whole heart and soul.

He snatched up the remote control and changed the television channel. The ball game wasn't helping. Maybe the evening movie would distract him. No, hell no...a love scene! He couldn't take *that*. How about the news? Lord, that could be worse. With his luck, they'd show her picture.

Just as he settled for a documentary about African iguanas, the doorbell rang. As much as he needed a distraction, he didn't want to answer it. The only person he wanted to see right now wouldn't be standing at his door.

The bell persisted, and with a soft curse, he trudged across the living room to answer it. Probably one of his investigators anxious to discuss a case.

He opened the door to find Hattie with a six-pack of beer in one hand, a bag of pretzels in the other, and a cigarette in her mouth. "Came to watch the ball game," she muttered as she pushed her way past him and into the living room.

"I'm not watching the ball game, Hattie," he said, remaining at the door, holding it open in hopes that she'd go back through it. "And I'm not in the mood for company."

She set the six-pack and pretzels down on a side table, then plopped herself into the armchair nearest the ashtray he always kept for her. "Okay, we won't watch the ball game. How 'bout a beer?"

"No, thanks." Reluctantly he closed the door and joined her in the living room. "If you think you're going to talk me into giving you those photos of Claire Richmond," he warned, settling down onto the sofa, "you're wasting your time."

She leaned forward in the chair, and he recognized the glint in her eyes. Something big was up. "I've been offered good money for those photos, T.K. Eight million dollars."

"Eight million! By whom?"

"A private individual—*not* a tabloid."

"The photos aren't for sale."

"This individual is willing to sign an agreement that they won't be published anywhere."

He frowned. "Why does this individual want them, then?"

"What difference does that make? Think about it, T.K. Eight million dollars, split down the middle, you and me."

"Forget it."

"Okay, you get sixty percent, I get forty."

"I'm not negotiating."

"Take it all, then. The whole eight million. I'll settle for the first year's interest."

"The photos are gone, Hattie. Gone. I burned them."

Silence descended between them. Tyce felt as if her gaze were examining his soul. "Oh, c'mon, T.K.," she finally chided, her voice unusually quiet. "We both know you didn't burn them."

He stared at her, perplexed by the sudden thickness in his throat. He hadn't destroyed the photos.

"You didn't burn them," she said gently, "because they're of her."

He sucked in a deep breath, rested his elbows on his outspread knees and rubbed his hands wearily over his face. He hated it when she was right. "You can't have the photos, Hattie," he told her in a bleak, hoarse voice. "For any price. Ever."

She leisurely smoked her cigarette and watched him. "Why not?"

Because they're all I have left of her. He swallowed the words to stop himself from saying them. "I don't want to take the chance that the photos will end up in some newspaper."

"So what if they do? That's why we took them, ain't it?"

"I won't do that to Claire. She'd be hurt all over again." Quietly, fervently, he added, "And I'd rather cut my heart out."

The declaration hung heavily in the air.

He hadn't meant to reveal so much, but her persistence had pushed him over some edge, and he felt as if he were hanging on to his discretion by the slimmest of threads.

Hattie promptly yanked on that thread. "You love her, don't you?"

He shut his eyes, struggling. "Yes," he whispered.

Surprisingly she had the sensitivity to fall silent as he worked to unclench the muscles in his throat. The silence didn't last nearly long enough. "Did you tell her?"

"No."

"Why not? Call her. Tell her."

His annoyance flared, coming to his rescue. "What good do you think it would do to call her?" he demanded harshly. "It wouldn't matter what I'd say. She'd only think I was after something—more photos, or her money."

"Neither sounds too bad to me. A billion dollars is nothing to sneeze at, T.K."

"A billion dollars," he repeated with loathing. "Know what I think of those billion dollars? If she had a weenie roast and burned the whole damn wad, I'd dance around the bonfire."

Hattie drew on her cigarette and blew out a few smoke rings.

"If she didn't have all that money," he went on, the anguish building inside of him, "there'd be nothing barring my way. I'd do whatever it took."

"To what?"

Embarrassed by what he'd already admitted, he turned away from Hattie's gaze, which suddenly struck him as somewhat calculating. As she ground out her cigarette, Tyce noticed another oddity—a small black hole in the side of the cardboard beer carton. Narrowing his eyes, he leaned forward to get a better look.

It wasn't just a hole, he realized. It was a *glassed-in* hole. Like...*a camera lens.*

With a growl, he launched off the sofa and grabbed the beer carton. Hattie let out a shriek and threw herself at him, trying to tug the weighty six-pack out of his hands. "Don't break the camera, T.K. It cost me a fortune!"

"Camera, hell! I should break your damn neck! Don't you have any decency at all? I can't believe that even *you*—"

"I *had* to do it, T.K.!"

"Had to do what?" he demanded. "Sell me out to a television tabloid? Freeze a few frames for your front page?" In tight-lipped disgust, he let go of the carton, allowing her to snatch it to her chest and stagger backward into the armchair. Lurching toward the front window, he jerked the draperies aside and peered through the summer twilight. Just as he'd suspected, a minivan with dark, tinted windows was parked across the street, beyond Hattie's car in his driveway.

A surveillance van, he had no doubt.

Cold with fury and the pain of betrayal, he strode across the living room, flung open his front door and marched across the lawn. Hattie followed him at a cautious distance. "Calm down, T.K. It's not what you think. You'd better let me explain."

He was beyond listening to explanations. She'd

betrayed him in a way he'd never forgive. He'd laid open his heart and given her just what she'd need to send the media into another frenzy over Claire. They'd have new reasons to hound her now…and to keep her name in the tabloid headlines.

He hadn't been lying. *He'd rather tear out his heart…*

Intending to toss aside whomever he found and destroy the video with his bare hands, he yanked open the side door of the van. A pale, wide-eyed woman loomed up before him, and he came to a sudden halt. His very heart thudded to a halt.

Good Lord… Had he become delusional?

Claire stood in the doorway of the van, her violet-blue eyes and spiky lashes glistening with tears in the dim light cast by a television screen.

He couldn't, for the life of him, move a muscle…or make sense of the bizarre situation. "What…what are you…"

"Turnabout's fair play," she whispered, dashing a single tear from the corner of her eye. "You spied on me—" her gaze caressed his face "—now I've spied on you."

A jumble of emotions clogged his throat as he struggled to believe it was true. She was here, in person, smiling at him through glistening tears, speaking in a voice as soft and tender as one of her kisses.

"Claire," he breathed, his hands sliding around her slender waist entirely of their own accord.

"I was thinking of holding a weenie roast," she whispered, twining her arms about his neck. "You know, burning my 'whole damn wad.' Thought you might like to come and, uh, dance around my bonfire."

The full implication sank in as the fog in his brain cleared away. She'd heard everything he'd said tonight—all the things he'd been longing to tell her.

"I'd burn all my money," she swore, "if I thought it was stopping you from loving me."

"Nothing can do that," he uttered fervently. "Nothing."

While emotion swelled too tightly in his chest to allow him to say anything more, he lifted her down from the van, locked her solidly into his arms and kissed her with all the gladness thrumming through him. Her response ignited an instantaneous heat, and he had to force himself to pull back from her to regain some semblance of control.

When finally he was able to talk, he whispered, "I've been meaning to speak to you about your last name. You've tried Richmond, and you've tried Jones. How about 'Walker'?"

She raised her brows in question. "You mean as in 'Mrs.'?"

"As in, Mrs. Tyce Walker."

She pretended to consider it, then pronounced, "It's me!" Her smile brimmed with love and joy and everything he'd ever wanted out of life. "It says everything I want my name to say."

He caught her to him in a vital kiss. She weaved her fingers through his hair and angled her face to pull him in deeper. He pressed her back against the van, provoking an even greater urgency between them.

She'd found love! she realized, dazed by her miraculous good fortune. She loved him completely, without reservation, without the slightest doubt that he loved her, too.

Her prayers at last had been answered.

"Come inside with me," he beckoned hoarsely, his body hard and needful of her. "I think we'd better do a body search to make sure you're not tagged. A very thorough search."

From the fire in his gaze, she knew he intended more of a "search and seizure." She liked the idea immensely.

He swept her off her feet and carried her into the house. Neither he nor she gave a thought to the queen of the tabloid press, armed with a loaded camera.

No reason that they should.

She'd already left...and without a single shot.

MEN at WORK

All work and no play?
Not these men!

July 1998
MACKENZIE'S LADY by Dallas Schulze

Undercover agent Mackenzie Donahue's
lazy smile and deep blue eyes were his best
weapons. But after rescuing—and kissing!—
damsel in distress Holly Reynolds, how could
he betray her by spying on her brother?

August 1998
MISS LIZ'S PASSION by Sherryl Woods

Todd Lewis could put up a building with ease,
but quailed at the sight of a classroom! Still,
Liz Gentry, his son's teacher, was no battle-ax,
and soon Todd started planning some
extracurricular activities of his own....

September 1998
A CLASSIC ENCOUNTER
by Emilie Richards

Doctor Chris Matthews was intelligent, sexy
and *very* good with his hands—which made
him all the more dangerous to single mom
Lizette St. Hilaire. So how long could she
resist Chris's special brand of TLC?

Available at your favorite retail outlet!

MEN AT WORK™

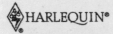 HARLEQUIN®    *Silhouette*®

Look us up on-line at: http://www.romance.net

PMAW2

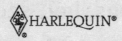

Not The Same Old Story!

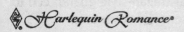

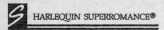

Glamorous, hot, seductive...

THE AUSTRALIANS

Stories of romance Australian-style guaranteed to fulfill that sense of adventure!

September 1998, look for
Playboy Lover
by Lindsay Armstrong

When Rory and Dominique met at a party the attraction was magnetic, but all Dominique's instincts told her to resist him. Not easy as they'd be working together in the steamy tropics of Australia's Gold Coast. When they were thrown together in a wild and reckless experience, obsessive passion flared—but had she found her Mr. Right, or had she fallen for yet another playboy?

The Wonder from Down Under: where spirited women win the hearts of Australia's most independent men!

Available September 1998 at your favorite retail outlet.

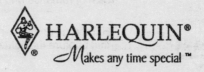

HARLEQUIN®
Makes any time special ™

Look us up on-line at: http://www.romance.net   PHAUS3

COMING NEXT MONTH

#697 A BODY TO DIE FOR Kate Hoffmann
Hero for Hire

When bodyguard Jackson Beaumont discovered he'd be guarding Judge Lamar Parmentier, he never suspected the judge was a corpse! Or that the late judge's widow would be so young, so gorgeous, so irresistible.... But Madeline Parmentier had a secret. And until Jackson figured out what she was hiding, he didn't dare trust her with his heart—or his life!

#698 TAKEN! Lori Foster
Blaze

Virginia Johnson ran a huge corporation—she was a woman in control. Until Dillon Jones—whose job description *wasn't* listed in the Fortune 500—kidnapped her. Suddenly she was at the mercy of a powerfully sexy man who kept her both captive...and captivated.

#699 SINGLE SHERIFF SEEKS... Jo Leigh
Mail Order Men

Single sheriff Dan Collins was seeking some peace and quiet. That ended when the townsfolk placed his personal ad in *Texas Men* magazine. Coincidentally, Dan stumbled upon his most bizarre case ever—and one very single sexy suspect. What could Dan do but stick *closer-than-this* to gorgeous Annie Jones?

#700 THE LAST BACHELOR Carolyn Andrews

Mac Delaney couldn't believe it—he'd lost all his poker buddies to matrimony! But Mac wasn't about to let any woman drag him to the altar *ever*. Then he met gorgeous Frankie Carmichael, and was ready to kiss the single life goodbye...till he discovered Frankie had *no* desire to walk down the aisle either!
